Night of Triumph

NIGHT OF TRIUMPH

Peter Bradshaw

Duckworth Overlook

First published in 2013 by
Duckworth Overlook
90-93 Cowcross Street, London EC1M 6BF
Tel: 020 7490 7300
Fax: 020 7490 0080
info@duckworth-publishers.co.uk
www.ducknet.co.uk

The right of Peter Bradshaw to be identified as the Author of
the Work has been asserted by him in accordance with
the Copyright, Designs and Patents Act 1988.

A catalogue record for this book is available
from the British Library

ISBN 978-0-7156-4501-7

Typeset by Ray Davies
Printed and bound in the UK by the
MPG Books Group, Bodmin, Cornwall

For Dominic

'Should we do anything? Should we do everything?'

Red Cross nurse in Portsmouth, upon hearing
the news of VE Day

One

It was not the King's custom to listen to wireless broadcasts in the presence of his family, but on Tuesday May 8th 1945, at 3pm, he was to be found doing so in a State Room in Buckingham Palace, along with Her Majesty The Queen, Her Majesty Queen Mary, the Princesses Elizabeth and Margaret, and his Private Secretary Tommy Lascelles, who stood throughout, having personally brought in the radio and adjusted it. The speaker was the Prime Minister, Winston Churchill:

Our gratitude to all our splendid Allies goes forth from all our hearts in this island and throughout the British Empire. We may allow ourselves a brief period of rejoicing, but let us not forget for a moment the toils and efforts that lie ahead. Japan, with all her treachery and greed, remains unsubdued. The injustice she has inflicted upon Great Britain and the United States, and other countries, and her detestable cruelties call for justice and retribution. We must now devote all our strength and resources to the completion of our task both at home and abroad. Advance, Britannia! Long live the cause of freedom! God Save The King!

The Prime Minister was succeeded here by a Home Service announcer, and at a nod from the King, Lascelles stepped forward and turned off the set. There was silence. The Princesses were clear-eyed, waiting for their father to speak: only Margaret's girlish, inattentive swinging of a foot signalled anything other than a solemn awareness of the occasion. Finally, the King grunted amiably and said to his wife:
'Spoke well, eh?'
'Oh yes.'

'Cadences. Such cadences. Forms of speech. Never heard anything like it before him.'

'Oh you have. His style is taken from Lloyd George.'

'Is it?'

'Bertie, don't be an ass, of course it is.'

Ping!

The weather was seasonable, and yet what Queen Mary felt in her hands and fingertips to be a coldness in the air caused one of her rings to slide off and hit the floor, before rolling away who knows where. On a less glorious day, she might have thought it ominous.

'Oh, oh dear,' Mary said in vexation. Lascelles stepped forward, but hesitantly, unsure if his help would be impertinent, conscious of a potentially catastrophic lowering of dignity on both his part and the Sovereign's, should she, through an awful sense of politeness, actually feel constrained to forestall him by going down on her hands and knees herself.

Both Princesses jumped up, grateful for something to do; they were soon scurrying about the floor as their parents talked calmly of the continuing war in Japan, and the coming years of peace. Margaret scampered along, in a showy way, as if childishly chasing a small kitten that she did not really want to catch. Often she would stand up, her fists on her hips, with a theatrical frown of concentration and annoyance. Mary herself had resumed her seat, apparently content that the girls would find her ring. A footman had been inaudibly called by the Queen, but at a gesture of dismissal from Mary, had vanished again.

Elizabeth looked for the ring in a far more methodical way, trying to judge the angle of departure from her grandmother's hand, lightly raking the floor with her fingers, remaining at ground level, looking along the carpet like a golfer judging the angle of a crucial putt. Where was it? The childish hide-and-seek impulse had come to her easily enough, heaven knows, and yet now she felt it burdensome. Something about being in the family – what her father had soppily called 'we four' – always caused her to revert to childhood, although she was fully nineteen years old, and as much of a grownup as any. Quite alone in this group, Elizabeth was in uniform: she was in the Auxiliary Territorial Services, the ATS. She wore the khaki belted tunic and skirt, khaki stockings and the cumbersome flat brown shoes. Not entirely unflattering to her figure, as she had had her dressmaker take in the tunic so that it was more waisted. In fact, Elizabeth privately believed that her uniform made her look more curvaceous than any of her civilian clothes, and this was an important part of the pride she took in it, though she would naturally never dream of admitting this to a living soul.

Yet Elizabeth glimpsed her profile at the bottom of a long mirror, and now feared that she looked merely a little girl playing some sort of dressing-up game. She was nineteen!

'Ha! Very good!'

The last speaker was Mary, because Margaret had now more or less forgotten about her ring, and was doing an impression of Charlie Chaplin's splay-footed waddle, having borrowed her grandmother's furled umbrella as a cane.

'Awfully good!'

Now her parents had noticed, and both applauded. Was Elizabeth expected to applaud too? If she continued to look for the ring and failed to clap, would she be told off for being grumpy and a bad sport?

Wait. *There* it was! Elizabeth could see it at the point of Margaret's Chaplin-cane, the umbrella, as if speared to the floor. Margaret had placed the point of the umbrella directly into it. She darted over and grasped the shaft of the umbrella and tried to pull it off. Margaret looked down, glanced at Elizabeth's annoyed face, knelt, flicked the ring into her left palm with one adroit movement and stood up.

'Grannie! I've found it!'

'Oh *well* done, Margo!'

'Jolly well done, Margaret Rose!'

Her parents joined in the exclamations, and her pretty face was showered with kisses. Elizabeth could tell, instantly, that her father loudly exaggerated his compliments to Margaret through irritation at Elizabeth's failure to congratulate her sister on finding the ring. Too big for her boots, was it? Lascelles, into whose ear a footman had just whispered, trundled the radio on castors over to him, and then stepped over to murmur something to Their Majesties. It was while they were all distracted that Elizabeth reached across and with the thumbnail and fingernail, both filed to an asymmetric point, nipped the loose, puckered flesh behind Margaret's right elbow. She did not draw blood, but pressed hard enough to make two red lines, like a tiny number eleven, visible on the flesh.

'Ow,' yelped Margaret, and at the same moment Elizabeth snapped 'Ow' herself, woundedly holding her own wrist, as the King and Queen sharply glanced in their direction. This was a piece of strategic cunning Elizabeth had developed in the nursery, in order to obscure the question of guilt, and to overwhelm the grownups with a weary reluctance to sort out who had started what.

'Come now, girls,' said the King, and allowed his sad, undeceived glance to rest on Elizabeth. To behave like babies, at their age. On this day, of all days. His eldest daughter was ashamed of herself, but vexed as well. When would they believe that she was a grownup? She had had military training. She had done her bit. And, though she hardly dared even to think about it, she would soon be engaged to be married.

No one dared think about it. A great number of influential people in Parliament and the Empire did not even know about it. Elizabeth's romance with Philip had been something which had first bemused her father, then worried him. He considered that an affair of the heart with a man she had first met when she was just thirteen years old signalled her naivety and vulnerability. Perhaps this romance, like so many of his subjects', had been dangerously accelerated by the war, and there had moreover been the unspoken possibility that Philip would be killed in action. But now the war was over; Philip had survived, and thinking about Elizabeth's marriage was something else that could no longer be put off.

The two girls lowered their eyes and dropped a tiny, propitiatory curtsey.

'Sorry, papa.'

Philip was still at sea in his ship, the *Renown*; Elizabeth had received another letter from him just that morning, full of baffling and yet inordinately sweet enthusiasm about the men and the ship, and what he imagined his future naval career to be. Philip would with great simplicity and directness use the words 'we' and 'us' in relation to all this. Elizabeth knew that she should feel her heart swell with joy.

And yet it did not.

She had actually quarrelled with Philip at their last meeting, and it was the thought of this that caused Elizabeth's tummy to contract with anxiety.

They had been at her cousin Marina's house, walking in the garden. Marina and the staff delicately withdrew to allow them some privacy. They were, of course, intensely, secretly excited. Could this be the conversation which would include a certain question?

Philip instinctively walked on ahead into the grounds. Elizabeth, just as instinctively, walked a pace or two behind. It was just the same when she went for walks with her father at Sandringham. She would allow him to forge ahead, to breathe, to think. Then she would find some pretext to catch up, to show him something she had found, to begin a conversation.

That day Elizabeth had not been able to think of anything, and just scampered up and tried to hold his hand. Philip allowed this easily enough, but did not interlace his fingers with hers.

They had walked on, to within sight of the old tennis court, with its sagging net and hulking roller.

'I say,' said Philip, 'shall we have a tennis court when we are married?'

Elizabeth's heart turned over, both with delight at the suggestion, and disappointment that Philip had still not actually proposed.

'Well, I don't know,' said Elizabeth, '*do* you want to get married?'

Instead of playfully shaming him into going down on one knee, as she had hoped that it might, the question appeared only to irritate Philip.

'Well of course I do!' he said sharply. 'Don't you?'

'Yes,' said Elizabeth plaintively. 'But you might ask a chap properly.'

Philip stopped, lightly took both her hands in his, and even cleared his throat.

'Lilibet,' he said, 'marry me.'

Not quite the question she had been hoping for, more a command from the bridge, but it would do. Without waiting for a reply, however, Philip raised a finger to forestall any other remark. For a moment, Elizabeth listened in the utter quiet.

'Listen,' he said. 'Do you hear that?'

'What?' asked Elizabeth, baffled.

'That. Do you hear that?'

Again, Elizabeth listened in the complete silence.

'It's a nightingale, isn't it? Or is it a lark?'

'Philip, what on earth are you talking about?'

'Well, I like that!' Philip suddenly exploded. 'Just when I'm being romantic, you … you can't even hear.' Philip pressed his lips together, and his great handsome head jerked across to the right, looking dismissively away, presenting her with his profile. Then he stormed back to the house.

Had there been a nightingale? Or a lark? Had there been something? Had she failed to hear something at this vital moment? Elizabeth felt that she would never cease to reproach herself. How awful.

All this was weeks ago. Of course, they had agreed to meet since then. There was no difficulty with their engagement, or as she preferred mentally to term it, their 'understanding', but she was still rather mortified. All this was difficult for Philip. He was, as her father put it to her, a 'man's man' and so a courtship would always be delicate. Their marriage itself would be delicate. And perhaps there had been a bird. Perhaps he had heard a bird. Perhaps she should have just said, yes, I hear a bird. To agree, to be agreeable, wasn't that the secret of marriage, of life itself? Oh, she hoped she hadn't ruined everything! And yet, it wasn't her fault.

Was it?

Two

... has inflicted upon Great Britain and the United States, and other countries, and her detestable cruelties call for justice and retribution. We must now ...

Mr Ware turned over in his single bed, half-listening to the wireless, entirely audible from the room next door. His pleasant drowsiness was marred only by the puffy, greasy eiderdown coming into scratchy contact with his unshaven face. Somehow the surface of that eiderdown stayed very cold, no matter what body warmth was available to it. Mr Ware sank back down into sleep.

He was dreaming that there was still a war on. It was a happy dream. He was dreaming of horseflesh. He was dreaming of his own flesh, and that of dozens of others. He could feel an unevenness under his feet: a roughness caused by rubble, bomb damage, dislodged bricks, great shards of shattered glass, cables, fire tender hoses. He could feel the soles of his boots on all this, and for him it was solid ground: it was where he could thrive. If the surface of the ground was going to become smooth again, well, that was a poor lookout for Mr Ware. There had been chances for him, these last six years. Opportunities. Already, at the age of twenty-six, he was richer than his father had ever been.

Mr Ware was not afraid of the war: he was not afraid of dying. On the contrary. Other people were afraid of dying when they saw him. He was not a violent man, but he carried a miasma of violence and chaos around with him, like the slipstream of a speeding, badly laden truck – the sort of truck, in fact, which was going to have its contents systematically looted when stationary at a depot.

Mr Ware smiled, at the water-level of waking.

... all our strength and resources ...

Yes, that was it. All his own strength and resources had been substantially deployed over the past few hours. But tonight was going to be his last chance. VE Night. A final bacchanal of wrong-doing. Mr Ware had never hated the Germans or the Japanese: it was a conviction that he had semi-seriously considered declaiming to the conchie board. But it was more, of course, that he didn't hate them any more than any other foreigner, or any more than men from Liverpool, or Glasgow, or people from south of the river, or people from the other side of the Kilburn High Road, or his wife.

The sharp contact of one of his vertebrae with that of someone else reminded Mr Ware that he was actually in bed with his wife. She had her back to him; they were curled foetally, away from each other, or as foetally as they could manage in such a narrow bed.

Mr Ware had had sex with three people in the past week, and none of them was his wife. She was always pestering him for conjugal relations. She'd wanted to get married when he got back from Italy. He had obliged. Now she wanted a baby. He had said all right. This theoretically meant refraining from all contraceptive procedures, but they had never used any in the first place, and this decision in fact coincided with the dwindling of their actual marital relations to zero. The business of trying for a baby seemed in practice to mean simply raising their levels of fretful resentment.

He was properly awake now: gazing at the ceiling, which bulged downwards like a shallow hammock, or, turning, he could look over at the wall, from where he could hear the wireless, or down at the floor's uncarpeted boards, where he could see the chamber-pot, with some sparkling droplets at its rim. Or over at the window dressing table where, in deference to his wife, Mr Ware had placed a stately three-glass mirror, a sort of hinged triptych, whose outer glasses could be swung in and out at various angles so that her hairdo could be objectively scrutinised. Mr Ware sometimes used it to inspect his bald patch. Like everything else in this flat, it was stolen.

Grumpily, he pulled the greasy, cold eiderdown over to his side some more, which disclosed his wife's naked legs, which had thin scars from where she had had to wear splints as a child – to cure rickets, she'd told him. He had never minded those.

Sleeping during the day had felt luxurious and dissolute at first. Now it was simply part of his working life. Working nights. Coming home in the gleaming dawn with full pockets, or a full car-boot. Caked with dust. Torn clothing. Off with the gear. Her job was to mend it. Part of her job anyway. Not that she was much good at that.

Mr Ware fell to wondering what the future held for them now. Perhaps London was no good. They could go to Brighton. Or Norwich. Mr Ware wondered, incuriously, what his wife felt about any of this: the possibility of her being obstructive, making trouble. He would want to do something, she would want something else. She would get in the way.

And of course she would still be on about this baby business.

Over the dressing table was his wife's collection of newspaper clippings about the Royal Family: George V, Mary, the current King and Queen, their two daughters. It was a mild obsession of hers. A piece of silliness. But it had sprung from something real enough. Ten years or so ago, Mrs Ware had been a girl, working in a canteen in the YMCA on Great Russell Street, a place with a sign outside saying 'Teas'. It was decent enough. Her mother, now late mother, had served behind the counter, and Mrs Ware had been allowed to help out, which she had loved – another part of her past Mr Ware didn't like, incidentally. It seemed to mean he was going to be expected to help her set up some similar joint after the war.

One afternoon, a woman had come in with two girls in tow. She was dressed like a sort of nanny or governess, and the two girls were looking around as if they'd never seen anything like it in their lives. The grownup had bustled forward and asked for one tea and two lemonades; Mrs Ware had instantly recognised the girls as Elizabeth and Margaret. The woman had plonked herself down at a table, expecting to be served; his mother-in-law had sharply told her she was supposed to collect the drinks herself, but Mrs Ware had brought the lemonades over, just so that she could lean across and touch the Princesses' hair. They had reacted as if a gorilla at London Zoo had reached through the bars and taken their ice cream. Her mother had come over and given her daughter a clip round the ear: for disobeying her order about the drinks, you understand, not touching the royal persons, whom she had not recognised.

But soon there had been uproar, as everyone gathered round their table, wanting to talk to them, shake their hand, touch them. Some chap with a camera had materialised out of nowhere and soon the woman and her charges had fled. Mr Ware smiled thinly at the memory, and the memory wasn't even his. That would teach them to try mingling with the common folk, wouldn't it?

Mr Ware got up, swung his legs over the edge of his high bed, stood, pulled his pyjama trousers up, shrugged on a dressing gown and went out of the bedroom, across the hall and into the bathroom, hearing the music from next door's wireless amplify briefly as he did so. He switched the light on with a long string cord, despite it being day: the building faced onto a high blank wall which blocked out the sun. The bulb gave the room a sickly yellowish wash.

He looked at his face: the sandy, receding hair, bags under the eyes, a slight squint. Instinctively, Mr Ware screwed up his eyes so that this face would go out of focus, went out to the lavatory to urinate, and then came back and filled up the handbasin for a shave, a basin which was supported from underneath by two wooden struts. The whole thing in the past year had almost collapsed. Mr Ware then brushed his teeth and went back to the lavatory, stood on the pan, removed the cistern's heavy china lid with much puffing effort and took out something encased in sacking. This he transferred to his dressing gown pocket, partly because it was too heavy and unwieldy to stay there, and partly because he just loved touching it.

Back to his room. His wife was still asleep. With a tenderness he never showed in the marital bed, Mr Ware laid his bundle down on the dressing table and unwrapped it: a Luger. The ugly, rectilinear form of a German pistol. He had been embarrassed about this possession in the last few months, sensing that it showed a want of patriotism. But now, on this day of all days, he considered that these worries were obsolete. Now was a time to show magnanimity to the defeated enemy, was it not? If it had been a Japanese gun, now that would be different.

Mr Ware pulled back the breech into its triangular hump with a click and for the thousandth time wondered, what would it be like? All those men that joined up and saw action – they must have wondered the same thing, Mr Ware thought. They must have wondered. What would it feel like? To be allowed to do that. He picked up the Luger and felt the serrations of all those tiny raised goose-pimple points of metal. It gave him a tingle which travelled up his forearm and into his right cheek.

Thirty-five shillings this thing had cost, with another five and six for the Sten gun ammo which he had in another bundle in the dressing table drawer.

He had only fired it once. The chap who had sold it to him had offered to take Mr Ware to Cambridge Heath in the early morning, to an out-of-the way spot, and let him have a bit of a bang. They'd actually had a couple of drinks the night before. All he'd wanted was to buy some liveners and here's this fellow asking him if he was in the market for a firearm. They'd gone to the cinema together after that: Abbott and Costello in *Here Come the Co-Eds*. Then lots more drinks at this club he knew about, and then in the grey light of dawn they'd gone out to this great big marshy place. He was still three sheets to the wind. Chap had stood behind him while he pulled the trigger. Ear-splitting crack and the recoil made his wrist feel like someone had hit it with a hammer. It wasn't like that in the films, was it? A real gun wasn't nearly as light as the toy pistol he'd once had. A real one weighed you down; it made you think about it all the time.

But still. After he'd shot it, Mr Ware had incautiously touched the hot barrel and pulled his fingers back. Ow. He'd tried twirling it round his finger like the cowboys and, once it had cooled down, shoved it into his belt like the American gangsters: it got a bit caught up in his shirt-tail. He and the chap had had a good laugh about that, and they fooled around a bit more. But when would he use it? Mr Ware supposed that it was tonight or never. He wrapped it up again and got ready to go out.

Three

'Oh lor', Hugh, I'm serious. Slow down.'

They were driving up Piccadilly, where the crowds in paper hats swarmed off pavements and up lampposts and, eager to focus their high spirits somewhere, they had pointed and cheered at Hugh's Lagonda all the way from the Ritz Hotel, where the two men had just drunk three cocktails each. Hugh cheerily waved and stamped on his accelerator, trying to deter revellers from actually jumping into the car with them. Taking the wheel with one hand, he shook out another couple of cigarettes from a packet and offered both to his passenger, and fellow Guards officer, Peter.

'Light one for me, would you?'

Hugh was master of the Old Etonian's art of never saying 'please'; Peter, an Old Carthusian, could never get the knack.

'Will you *please* slow down?'

A lady and her elderly mother actually jumped out of the way of the Lagonda, just as they reached Swaine Adeney Brigg, where Peter's mother had once bought him an umbrella, one which a girl had later borrowed and never returned. The memory swam into his mind at the same moment that the sun went briefly behind a cloud. It surely couldn't rain tonight, could it?

They stopped at a red light.

'These people – these are the people we've been fighting for,' said Peter piously, looking about him.

'Polish, are they?' said Hugh.

Peter merely frowned and looked over, disapprovingly, at Fortnum and Mason, where once, over tea, a girl had slapped his wrist when he had reached over and put his hand on her knee, at precisely the same table where twelve years previously his mother had smacked his hand for trying to take an extra profiterole.

He had lit both cigarettes and passed one to Hugh, who drew on it heavily. A woman and a younger man, perhaps her son, were waltzing across the road, apparently in spontaneous response to a man playing the accordion on the opposite side. There were many more cheers at this. The man was wearing a bowler hat which was splodged with paint in apparently random patterns but which, on closer inspection, revealed themselves to be an attempt to figure the Union Jack. The car lurched forward again, and Peter put his cigarette down, at knee level, now a little nauseous.

'Peter, my dear fellow,' said Hugh, 'I need you on your most sparkling form tonight. We have a very important task to perform.'

'What sort of task?'

'A pastoral task. We shall be *in loco parentis*. And *in loco* a lot of other things besides. No, I'm awfully sorry, no.' This last was to a boy who had asked for a cigarette.

'What do you mean?'

'We are to be chaperones. Squiring a couple of girls about. Nothing too taxing.'

'I thought we were going to the Club.'

'We may very well be going to the Club. But during tonight's festivities, we shall be showing these two young women the capital.'

'Are they foreigners?'

'They have some German ancestry, but no, they are as British as you and me. They have, as it were, been through London but never actually into the streets. That's where you and I come in.'

They were now opposite Simpson's, where Peter's mother had once bought him a three-piece suit and topcoat, and where his former fiancée had looked at a tray of silver tie-pins, cuff-links and money-clips, looked up at Peter, burst into tears, run out through the back entrance into Jermyn Street and never contacted him ever again. He was wearing the suit now.

Some ten minutes later, Hugh and Peter arrived at their shared service flat in Oxendon Street. Hugh was running a bath, and padding about the place with a vivid white towel around his waist. Peter was thoughtfully looking out of the window. They both had drinks.

'Are we going to be up terribly late tonight, do you think?'

'Up *late*?' Hugh looked up from the electric fire, one of whose glowing orange bars he had effortfully turned on by a switch at the side. 'My dear boy, we are going to be up all night. It's going to be back here for breakfast, absolutely roaring. It's going to be like Eights Week.'

He disappeared into the bathroom, where the sound of running water ceased and there was a sploshing as Hugh disturbed the water's surface with his finger tips. Peter made no reply, but continued to look out of the window.

'Look at the crowds. Extraordinary. And do you know, I don't see a single policeman. The wireless said there wasn't an inch of space outside the Palace. People everywhere. Father said it reminded him of the General Strike, only we're all on the same side. What's this thing?'

Peter had picked up a large portfolio in green leather, secured with two tied tassels, which he began to undo.

'Hugh, what's this folder thing? Have you been making sketches of Rheims Cathedral or somesuch?'

Peter undid the second tassel, and opened it up to see the photographs inside, just as Hugh, naked, dripping and unsmiling, cannoned into him and furiously snatched the portfolio. Without looking at Peter, he stalked back into the bathroom and locked the door shut behind him.

'I wouldn't have thought that sort of thing was your taste, old boy,' said Peter at the bathroom door, attempting to be worldly and amused, although in truth this manner did not suit him and he rather wanted to be told that this portfolio did not belong to Hugh. As if divining this need, Hugh opened the door again and appeared in a damp burgundy dressing gown.

'It is not mine. It's a friend's,' he said, shortly. 'I didn't know what was inside. I wouldn't dream of making free with someone else's property.'

Back on the defensive, Peter made a grimace of concession, walked back into the sitting room and resumed his survey of the crowds as they surged through into Leicester Square. Trying to rejoin the celebratory mood, he hummed along to the song they were all singing.

'Bloody hell,' said Hugh at his shoulder, his dyspeptic humour apparently dispelled and thoughts of a bath apparently delayed. 'I call that disloyalty to the human race. If the bloody thing did manage to run away, and the farmer didn't get his wretched rabbit pie, we would all bloody well starve. Here.'

Hugh passed Peter a copy of the *Daily Express*, unfolded at an inside page.

'There you are.'

'What?'

'Take a look.'

Hugh looked, but all he could see was a photograph of the Royal Family.

'What is it?' he asked, mystified.

'Our target for tonight, old boy,' said Hugh. 'Our mission. There are the two girls we're taking out.'

Uncomprehending, Peter looked back at the photograph, and then around the margins of the page, searching for details that could possibly apply to him, then looked back at the picture. He looked back suddenly at Hugh, who laughed shrilly.

'I see the penny has dropped, like a manhole cover released from an upstairs window.'

'You don't mean?'

'I do mean.'

'How ...?'

'Mother. She had the call from St James's. This is a great honour for us, old thing. This is something to tell our grandchildren about. Authorised version, naturally. Should I top that up, before we venture out?'

Both resplendent in the uniform of the Scots Guards, Peter

and Hugh were soon walking down the street, bestowing beaming smiles on everyone they saw. They were moving far more quickly than in the car. The crowds parted for them. They were actually being cheered. It was the way they were dressed, naturally, and something to do with their ferociously brushed hair, each in a razor-sharp side-parting: Peter's dark, Hugh's sandy-blond.

Hugh had it in mind to stop for a pint at a pub, but they made time for an American newsreel camera crew, and a woman with chic cropped hair, interviewing passers-by.

'Do you think the war changed the British view of America?' she asked.

'I think it has very much reinforced it,' replied Hugh, with a perfectly courteous smile.

'Do you think the war has changed the British relationship with America?'

'Oh, we are as close as cousins.'

'And who is your favourite American motion picture star?'

'I would say Lou Cost–'

Hugh was interrupted by a football from an impromptu game outside a café, which struck him unpleasantly on the back of the neck. Livid, he turned around to see that the majority of the players were policemen, the first he had seen on duty that day. They cheered and motioned for him to throw it back. Mastering his anger, aware that the cameras were still rolling and that the American interviewer's amused gaze was still on him, Hugh affected a hearty, tolerant laugh and threw the ball back to them, swinging his arms from the side, however, as if making a rugby pass.

'There.'

Five minutes later, they had come back to a pub quite near Piccadilly Circus: the Captain's Cabin. They both ordered pints of warm, brimming Bass and these, as well as the warm cheers their uniforms elicited, restored their good humour.

'I say, I'm rather looking forward to tonight. When should we arrive at the Palace?' asked Peter, but this last word showed a want of discretion and Hugh frowned. His eyes flickered around the bar in which they were the centre of attention and he shook his head minutely.

'Soon. Soon.'

Peter looked at his watch. The frosted glass of the pub, chased with Edwardian advertisements of ales and fortified wines, was darkened with a press of people, all excited by each other, all wanting their gathered force to cohere into one great moment. This was what his father had told him about 1926, the General Strike. They eavesdropped on the conversation at the next table.

'What are you going to do now, Bill?'

'Well, I expect Laura and I can get married.'

'Oh, jolly good. In Saxmundham?'

'That all depends.'

'Harry back?'

'No. Still in Singapore. Hasn't got his demob papers. Could be another year.'

'Do you know what John's last letter said?'

'No. What?'

'Said his CO asked him, are you a communist or just a trouble-maker?'

'What'd he tell him?'

'Bit of both. Cheer-o!'

Under their feet was a continual grinding and scrunching of glittering grit, from the heels and soles of newly polished shoes; people slid back and forth to the bar with drinks and orders for drinks, sometimes coming back to tables in the Saloon Bar with full glasses on round tin trays. The upright piano in the corner had its lid pulled up by one man who, with two fingers, plunked out a children's tune on the black notes.

Oh, will you wash my father's shirt?
Oh, will you wash it clean?
Oh, will you wash my father's shirt –
And hang it on the green?

A cheer and a groan. Someone else took over, rolling up his sleeves, meshing his fingers together and bending them out backwards until they all cracked. Then he played 'Roll Out The Barrel' and Hugh joined in cheerfully, and Peter did his best, smiling thinly and uncertainly. He didn't know any of the words, other than those which were in the title.

'Hugh. *Hugh.*'

'Mm?'

'I, ah, where's the …?'

'Over there.'

He pointed to a door round by the other side of the bar, so low and unostentatious, Peter assumed it must be a locked store cupboard. He placed his lit cigarette in the ashtray and sidled through the press with his palms raised and head tilted back, as if gracelessly performing the preliminary moves in some sort of mambo.

After a futile shove, and then a pull, the door opened onto a descending staircase, almost entirely dark, which led to a dank room. As the door to this shut firmly behind him, Peter was confronted by a stooping man in a chalk-stripe suit, with a large, balding head and an ingratiating smile: simply standing there. A length of white shirt-tail protruded from his fly-buttons.

'Hello,' he said.

Peter considered briefly pretending to have forgotten something – perhaps accompanying this with a snap of the fingers and a pantomimed vexed expression, before turning to flee back up the stairs. But the man stepped away from the urinal, and motioned for Peter to approach.

'I do apologise,' he said, and then, 'Do you have the time?'

Peter found it difficult to urinate in front of other people at the best of times. It was the sort of thing which, unfairly, aroused suspicion in the services, as if you were a moral danger to your brother officers. He frowned, looked down, and ducked into the single, enclosed cubicle. Peter closed the door behind him, but was afraid to lock that, in case he was trapped. By pressing against it with his outstretched, tensed fingertips, he was able to keep the door secure while he relieved himself. After finishing, he listened. There was nothing outside but a dripping, foul-smelling quiet. Gradually, Peter relaxed. His breathing rate slowed. He stopped trembling. He calmed. He looked around at the words crudely scrawled on the walls, and smiled. Peter adjusted his dress, pulled the chain, and opened the door.

'I said – *do you have the time?*' said the man evenly, still there, his smile still in place, as if easy-going and tolerant of Peter's caprice.

Peter pushed past him, suppressing a thin squeak of anxiety, and began to wash his hands. This he made take longer than usual, and when he looked up, the man had gone. Sternly resolving to leave this place, and worrying that both their uniforms were going to get stained in some way, Peter marched back up the stairs and into the crush by the bar. 'Jerusalem' was now being played on the piano, to a storm of whistling. He mambo-ed back round to their table, to discover the very same man again, seated with his back to him, and in intimate conversation with Hugh.

'Ah, Peter,' said Hugh cheerily, 'this is Colin Erskine-Jones. A capital fellow I've just met.'

Colin turned and rose to shake Peter's hand. His manner had changed, perceptibly. The ingratiating manner had been removed; in its place was a smooth condescension.

'We've not been introduced,' he said, ambiguously.

'How do you do?' said Peter.

Without replying directly to this, Colin turned back to Hugh.

'Well, war work, you know,' he said, evidently in answer to a previous question. 'I actually volunteered for the ARP.'

'Really?' It was unusual for Hugh to appear surprised at anything, and Peter noted it.

'Oh yes. Really.'

'Clearing bomb damage and so forth?'

'Quite. Some of the chaps used to come straight from the regular jobs, work all night, and then go back to the office the next day with never a wink of sleep.'

'Marvellous. But wasn't it frightfully dangerous?'

'Oh, yes. But rewarding.'

Colin accompanied this last remark with an enigmatic smile, that both men found supercilious.

'Can I get you another?'

'Oh now, Hugh, surely we have to push on, rather?'

The extraordinary honour that had been conferred on them by this evening's 'chaperoning' duty, and the necessity of not making a mess of things, pressed on Peter's mind.

'Oh, Peter, don't be a wet blanket. We're in no great rush.'

'It's already twenty past.'

'So you *do* have the time.'

Simply to get away from Colin, Peter glumly volunteered to get three gins, threaded his way back to the bar, and made a fat and grimy tube with his coins while waiting to be served. A thin man with a pink face – the colouring was, on closer inspection, caused by a widespread latticework of infinitesimally fine broken veins – listened to his order with a lizardly flick of his eyes in Peter's direction and then, without making any effort to pour out the drinks, resumed his conversation.

'We mustn't let our guard down. We mustn't just slack off.'

'Oh no.'

'No.'

'We have to continue the battle in the Far East. The Japanese.'

'It makes my blood boil to think how they treated our chaps.'

'We wouldn't have treated *them* like that.'

'Ah well, it'll soon come. Victory in Japan. And then this will all be over.'

'Victory in Japan …' murmured someone into his Guinness.

'Victory in Japan,' said someone else, raising his glass, as if proposing a toast.

'Ah, yes. It's a good life, you know, as long as you don't weaken.'

This was an unfortunate moment for Peter to feel slightly dizzy, and to slump against the bar. He should have had something more to eat before he came out. A good life if you didn't weaken? What on earth did that mean? In what sense did being strong make it a good life? How?

'Shall I carry the gins for you?' said the pink-faced man suddenly, and his open contempt, and that of his fellows, made Peter pull himself together and refuse the request. He still did not quite understand that his uniform was triggering conversations about the war everywhere within earshot.

Peter returned to his table, to find a girl on Hugh's knee, talking to an older woman. Colin was in tears, having apparently broached the subject of what on earth he was going to do in peacetime. It was a melancholy theme, and Peter was to discover that a good deal of that night's merry-making was being indulged in all over London to avoid thinking about it.

'The wine business is in an awful state, old chap.' Colin had been a wine importer before the war.

'Mm,' said Hugh.

'The disruption on the Continent has of course wrought havoc with supply, and that naturally has taken prices up.'

'Mm.'

'But this only benefits those chaps with a serious holding of stock, a wide client base, or a good deal of capital. Or all three. I've got none.'

'Ah.'

'Perhaps I'll chuck it in, and go in for importing lightbulbs. Yet that, as you probably know,' he added, with infinite, tender sadness, 'has its own potential for heartbreak.'

'Yes,' said Peter.

'I see you were admiring my cigarette case,' Colin then said, producing the case and waving it about. 'I don't mind telling you I won't really need it for much longer, because – starting tomorrow – I am giving up smoking. Would you like to buy it?'

'What?'

'My cigarette case. Solid silver, you know. Make me an offer.'

'I don't really ...'

'I say,' said Hugh, decisively changing the subject. 'Let's sing a song. Here's one I've learned from other ranks!' He started to joggle his knees up and down, which made the girl on his knee and her friend splutter and giggle:

Bumpity-bumpity-bumpity-bump,
As if I was riding me charger!
Bumpity-bumpity-bumpity-bump,
Just like an Indian Rajah!
All the girls declare,
He's a gay old stager.
Hey! Hey! Clear the way,
Here comes the galloping Major!

Hugh concluded by giving his girl a candid and passionate kiss, which went on for some time; this appeared neither to interest nor to scandalise the company. Peter looked at his watch.

'I say, Colin,' said Hugh, breaking off from his kiss, struck by a sudden thought, 'were you saying something about getting married?'

This was another disagreeable subject, evidently, although it made their guest testy and defensive, rather than maudlin.

'I was; I mean, I am,' he replied. 'But my fiancée became rather a bore about my interests here in town.'

'She would rather live in the country?' inquired Peter, politely.

'It's partly that. I wouldn't mind. I could come up to town every week or so and stay at the Club. But she became very silly about some of my ... some of my *haunts*, you know.'

'Ah,' said Hugh, and winked.

'Ah,' said the girl on his knee, and winked as well, causing a gust of laughter among her friends.

'Some of my *interests*,' continued Colin gloomily, as if to himself, ' ... some of the things a chap has to do to blow off steam. My artistic side.'

With a deafening crash, a woman dressed as Britannia carrying a papier-mâché trident, and accompanied by a man in a mangy fur and a lion's head, entered the pub and began to sing

'Land Of Hope And Glory'. Through the open door, Peter could see how extraordinarily crowded the streets now were. He wondered if this would impede their journey to the Palace. For the first time, he wondered if Hugh had simply made up this story for a prank. Did he want to go somewhere else, in uniform like this? Peter felt a chill.

'Of course, the war has offered some opportunities,' Colin went on, in a confiding tone. 'One has had some chances to make money. In fact, I have a chance tonight to make rather a lot of money. One hardly likes to talk about it, and I probably *wouldn't* talk about it if I wasn't so tight.'

Peter was entirely indifferent to this man's financial problems, and could only nod, sipping joylessly at his gin and desperately trying to catch the eye of Hugh, who was now showing his girl a silver fob watch, periodically returning it to his pocket and inviting her to retrieve it, all as if emphasising his staggeringly casual attitude to the time. But then Hugh glanced sharply up at Peter and Colin.

'Yes, yes, yes,' he said. 'Don't be so *wet*. We're going now. We won't be late.'

He turned back to his girl and apologetically began the process of dislodging her from his lap.

'Salvage work, you might call it,' continued Colin dully.

'Shipping, you mean?' enquired Peter.

Hugh was now standing up, brushing his uniform with his fingertips; guiltily, Peter began to do the same thing.

'Time to be off, ladies,' said Hugh, and shrugged off the chorus of disappointment. Standing, both men continued to command the same attention as before. It was such an extraordinary thing to see men of their rank here, and the entire company took it as proof that anything went on this remarkable day.

Outside, the crowds were even more densely packed. There was bunting hung up everywhere and slogans. 'God Save The King' read one, and another, evidently an old placard, showed a picture of Marshal Stalin with the words, 'Second Front Now'.

The men were, as before, cheered and clapped on the back as they passed through. They would certainly have to walk to the Palace now.

Everywhere, faces: drawn faces, pale faces, lined faces, fat faces, like faces of an underground race temporarily permitted to take the air, in return for millennia of passivity. They sang, they whistled and laughed, they coughed and unselfconsciously spat on the ground. People gave each other the thumbs-up and seized upon the diversion that Hugh and Peter provided as they walked along. Some couples gazed into each other's eyes; others kissed. Everywhere, total strangers were hugging each other. Peter was quite certain that Hugh had insisted on their uniforms precisely to deter this kind of embrace.

Suddenly, there was a deafening explosion. Hugh's face went pale and taut, and so did everyone else's in the vicinity. But it was just a firework, let off in a doorway. The perpetrator grinned, and everyone cheered. Nobody was the least bit angry with him.

Four

Elizabeth's governess Bobo said that she had never seen so many people. Elizabeth said solemnly that she agreed, though in her heart she did not. There was indeed a sea of people outside the Palace and all the way down the Mall, but Elizabeth had witnessed the amazing spectacle before, after her father's Coronation, and two years before that, for her grandfather's silver jubilee; in fact, it seemed to her that there had been an enormous crowd out there in the Mall all her life. She assumed that a packed mass was its natural condition, which for some reason it somehow rarely achieved, and the usual lesser throng was just a dilution of its truer, denser state. They were like the crowds following Moses in the Book of Exodus which she had read and re-read as a girl.

Her mother took Elizabeth's hand quite sharply, almost pinching her palm, and did the same to Margaret on the other side.

'Ready?' she asked.

Four abreast, they walked forward and their formation straggled diagonally out into a line as they went through a heavy curtained canopy, and then reassembled into a single rank on the balcony to wave to the crowds. The response was not immediate. Her mother began to wave, and then her father, and then, shyly, the two daughters.

As the throng realised that what they had longed for had come to pass, a wave of cheering swept forward, although the actual volume did not seem to increase by very much. Elizabeth fancied she could see some in the crowds with telescopes and field glasses.

Elizabeth was not very used to acclaim. In the nursery, good behaviour was rewarded only with relatively curt and restrained gestures of approval from Bobo and the girls' nanny Crawfie, and it did not take Elizabeth long to work out that they themselves were soliciting approval from her mother. In the Auxiliary Territorial Service, her skills at driving and examining an engine were greeted with brisk and solemn nods and the occasional, excruciatingly self-conscious 'jolly good' from her instructors, wary of being accused by their fellows of sucking up – as she soon realised. Now, in her young womanhood, both her parents seemed cautious with her, as if with a racehorse in which they had over-invested. And as for Philip, her overt demand for his approval, for his love, had been badly misjudged. The memory of it snagged at her mind, like a thorn at her skirt. How could she keep thinking of that, on today of all days?

The crowd swarmed and fizzed and bubbled. What were they all thinking? One year ago, while her father was in Italy on a visit to the Eighth Army, Elizabeth's duties as a Counsellor had included signing the reprieve for a murderer. She wondered if that man was out there at this moment waving at her, now leading an entirely blameless and reformed life.

Her father, she knew, was nervous of both heights and crowds. Was this an awful trial for him? Austerely, Elizabeth severed the indulgent line of thinking as irrelevant. His Majesty was entirely indifferent to personal discomfort. This was a glorious day. She wondered if she might look around and smile at him, but had been warned that was incorrect; the proper form for balcony appearances was to keep facing outwards, as if for a portrait.

Elizabeth made some discreet adjustments to her uniform. She smoothed her skirt, pulled at the jacket sleeves, and with two little flicks at her hair, fully revealed the new earrings that Philip had bought for her. This had been some months ago. So far, he had got her nothing on the occasion of her engagement, and there was no question of a ring, because the understanding was not public yet. Now the earrings were fully visible, and the crowd gave a deafening throaty roar. Elizabeth was most gratified. She always knew that her earrings were attractive, and rather special, but never guessed that they would go down so well with the crowd. Beamingly, she turned to the left, and then to the right, to showcase each in turn; the crowd almost screamed and Elizabeth was thrilled that London adored them so much. She leaned over and was about to murmur something to this effect to her mother – who had in fact advised against wearing these earrings – when she saw Mr Churchill standing on the balcony next to her father.

He was wearing a bow tie, and had one arm aloft, an unlit cigar wedged into his middle and index finger, which were in the characteristic 'V' form. Instantly, Elizabeth and the rest of her family assumed benign, indulgent expressions which were invisible to the crowd, and indeed to Mr Churchill himself who appeared indifferent to those who had accorded him this singular honour. He was plainly ecstatic. He looked tired and very old to Elizabeth, but somehow also quite rejuvenated by the experience, like a character in a book by H. Rider Haggard that she had once read in the nursery.

Elizabeth knew how keenly her mother must have felt the discomfort of having the Prime Minister appear next to them out here, however admired he was by the people, by the Americans, and in the press. She did not care to appear on stage in a supporting role, and perhaps Mr Churchill himself realised this, because with a deep bow both to her father, and then to her mother, he absented himself from the balcony, and Elizabeth fancied his rejuvenation-thrill was heightened as the crowd's roar unmistakably lessened on his departure. She could see the jaunty spring in his step.

They carried on waving. Elizabeth knew that they must go in soon, and unlike Mr Churchill, did not particularly want to stay out there: no longer than was necessary, at any rate. They might need to go back out in an hour or so.

Elizabeth was wondering what she might do for the rest of the evening. Perhaps supper with Margaret, and then listen to a concert on the wireless. She was actually rather tired.

When they came back inside, Mr Churchill was there again, talking to one of his ministers, a taller man who had to bow a little to maintain the intimate, gossipy, murmuring exchange that Elizabeth knew all politicians liked to affect, even or especially if they had nothing of consequence to say: a display of importance and intrigue for other people's benefit. They broke off as the family re-entered the room and looked at them with a courtier-like attention: smiling, expectant, ready to speak if called upon and yet not forcing their presence on Their Majesties in any way. The cheering from outside was still entirely audible.

The Queen approached the Prime Minister, whose companion instantly withdrew.

'Well, Mr Churchill,' said the Queen in a high, clear, pleasant voice, 'you are one of the *political immortals* now!'

'Anyone who has suffered from insomnia will already know what immortality is, ma'am,' replied Churchill smilingly, with a bow.

The Queen was displeased with this conceited riposte; surely what was required of the Prime Minister was a simple and gracious thank you for the remarkable compliment she had just paid him, and which she had spent some minutes thinking up. There was an uncomfortable silence, which the King cheerfully interrupted.

'Jolly good! *Jolly* good! I can't think of a night like it!' he beamed around at the company. Mr Churchill and others bowed again. 'No,' he repeated, 'not a night like it. What a wonderful day in our history. And I believe we owe it all to you, Prime Minister.'

Churchill bowed again and his cadences then assumed the rise and fall which the King had praised earlier: 'Sir, I believe we owe it all to the lion-hearted fighting men and women of land, sea and air, who ...'

'All to you,' repeated the King happily. 'To think, it might have been Hitler and Eva Braun out there on the balcony – can you imagine? – or, or Von Ribbentrop, or ...'

Nobody cared to imagine. If things had been different, if

things had gone another way ... it was an ugly and futile line of thought.

The King was distracted by a murmured comment in his ear from the Queen, who had apparently been petitioned on a personal matter by her younger daughter. He listened with the cheery facial expression left over from his previous comment; presently, his face became blank as he considered this new topic and then became cheery again.

'Yes. Yes! Why on earth not? Lilibet!'

'Yes, Papa?'

'Your mother has told me about this plan of Margo's and yours!'

What plan? Elizabeth looked over at Margaret and was silently infuriated to see that she was putting on her 'innocent' face – lips compressed, gazing blandly up at a corner of the ceiling – copied from Minnie Mouse in a film show that they had seen at Windsor.

'I think it's jolly good,' continued the King; his mood of fatherly indulgence now had a boisterous, almost euphoric quality. 'As long as you're not out for too long, and you stay with these two chaps, then yes, jolly good. Be back in a couple of hours or so.'

What plan?

Margaret now approached her and had the grace to look sheepish.

'Lilibet, I thought it would be fun to go out tonight, sort of *incognito*! I knew Mama would never let me go on my own, so ...'

'So you told her it was my idea.'

'Oh *do* let's go out, Lilibet; it will be *such* fun. We've got Hugh and Peter coming with us, and you know as well as I do that we'll never be able to square Mama and Papa ever again. It's now or never.'

The full significance of what Elizabeth had been coerced into was only now dawning on her. She was going to go on a raucous evening out, what the Americans called a 'double date', with two young men – a daring adventure of the sort she had never experienced with her fiancé, and never expected to. What would Philip say when he found out? She did not doubt the probity of their chaperones for a moment. Indeed, she was incapable of questioning the motives of anyone who came into contact with her.

But she knew her mother had been hoping that the King would forbid this adventure, or at least would be unconvinced, so that his wife would have the casting vote of disapproval. Nobody had expected that he would be quite so enthusiastic and issue what amounted to a command. She knew her father well enough to realise that the fact that Margaret was a minor actually counted in the scheme's favour. She was still a child; in his heart, the King thought of Elizabeth as a child too, and so being out with a pair of responsible male adults could do no harm.

Margaret was now by the door, beckoning frantically, and with a facial expression somewhere between a grin and a wince. She knew quite well that every moment now spent in their mother's company might cause her to persuade the King against this plan. Bobo and Crawfie both stood behind her, each with a face like thunder.

With a curtsey – her parents broke off from conversation with Mr Churchill to nod in return – Elizabeth left the room and began to walk down the corridor with Margaret, exchanging little blows, kicks and slaps.

'Beast.'

'Pig.'

'Sneak.'

'Wet blanket.'

'Girls.'

Crawfie's thin voice cut in. There was a moment's quiet.

'Who *are* these men, anyway?'

Margaret's smile was complacent, as if she could never be caught out on such an obvious technicality.

'Hugh's a cousin of Lady Fermor's – you know, mama's lady-in-waiting. And Peter's his friend.'

The corridor was gloomy. All the windows were still cardboarded up, in case the glass was blown in by a bomb attack – the Palace had been a key target – and two lightbulbs in three had been removed for reasons of economy. The Queen loved economy, loved discussing it, worrying about it, enforcing it. Economising was not a pose with her. Peacetime would deprive her of much pleasure.

Accelerating, the Princesses rounded a corner, clatteringly descended a flight of stone steps, went down another passage and out into a courtyard. Hugh and Peter, their consorts for the evening, were waiting for them there, in the company of three civilian police officers. Hugh had a brilliant, reassuring smile which Peter was attempting to mirror, intended to announce the evening's mood of raillery and good humour. The policemen just looked blank and tense.

Elizabeth thought their companions for the evening were terribly handsome, and people who had never seen her close up were surprised by how attractive she was. As she approached, and secured a delicate bow from each man, Elizabeth sensed that this was particularly the case with Peter, rather sweetly shy and less relaxed than Hugh. She wondered which of the two she was supposed to be paired off with, a question smartly answered when Margaret curled her arm through Hugh's.

'Now, *I've* got a plan,' Margaret announced, and from a pocket took out two pairs of stage spectacles, props from their family pantomime production of *Puss In Boots* at Windsor Castle. They actually had plain glass. Elizabeth and Margaret both put them on, and instantly had a busybody-ish, American air. The two men laughed uncertainly, but Elizabeth sensed that the effect was strange and surreal rather than funny. She wanted a mirror, but nobody had one.

'Are we ready?' asked Hugh briskly.

'Rather!' said Margaret.

'Absolutely,' said Elizabeth.

Peter just nodded. Reflexively, the four of them linked arms, as another officer on duty opened a side gate and they streamed through it: rather as she had gone out onto the balcony, single-file and then a straggling line. Elizabeth found herself grinning and ducking as she emerged, as if under a rain shower or a handful of confetti. And she had gone into a trot, as if trying to reach some enclosure a few yards away. But of course there was no enclosure. This was it. She was outside. Elizabeth slowed down, to let the others catch up with her.

Even she could see that everyone, absolutely everyone, was drunk. People reeled and staggered. They lurched. A number, civilians and military, saw her uniform and saluted. Within the first minute, one man came lumbering up to Elizabeth for a kiss; his mouth was puckered up in a way that turned his lips into a tiny pale rosebud. He tripped over his own shoelaces and crashed to the ground fully twenty yards away, and was picked up under his armpits on either side by two men who looked like the Military Police. Close enough to startle all four, and on the other side of them, a man played 'God Bless The Prince of Wales' on his harmonica. A number of people had climbed to the very top of lampposts and were shouting 'Hurrah!' over and over again. Elizabeth thought it quite the most amazing thing she had seen, and the cheering buzzed inside her skull like a swarm of bees. Hurrah, hurrah, hurrah!

The man who had fallen over appeared now to have fainted, and was being dragged along by his friends while his knees and toes trailed feebly along the pavement. He crumpled entirely; his shoulders heaved, and a policeman asked if everything was all right. Another top-hatted man, who looked like a bishop, was walking purposefully over from a different direction, apparently to ask the same question.

Margaret whispered something in Hugh's ear. He grinned, and Margaret scampered up behind the policeman. Elizabeth held her breath, unable to credit what was clearly about to happen. Margaret raised her hand, and then with an almighty forward swipe – so that it would not be immobilised by the chinstrap – knocked off the policeman's helmet so that it fell over his face, and then reached over and grabbed it with both

hands. She turned around, pointed at the approaching bishop
and squealed loudly:

'He did it! The blackguard!'

Then Margaret tucked the helmet under her arm and called
out to the others:

'Run!'

They ran; the furious policeman was about to give pursuit
when the prostrate man groaned and slumped down further.
The officer realised that he had no choice but to stay with him.
The bishop now slowed to a halt, perhaps wondering if the
policeman would indeed suspect that he had something to do
with this affray, and then walked thoughtfully in another
direction.

After some minutes of running and dodging through the
mob, Elizabeth, Margaret, Hugh and Peter found themselves in
the gloaming of St James's Park. Breathless, sweating and unable
to speak, they just stared at each other. Finally, Margaret felt
sure enough of her prize and her safety to take the helmet out
from under her arm and put it on. She instantly puffed out her
cheeks, raised her right palm in a 'stop traffic' gesture and
with the other mimed putting a whistle to her lips, and did a
pompous, waddling march back and forth. The two men
behaved as if they thought it was the funniest thing they had
ever seen. So did many raucous passers-by. Peter's laugh was
the more nervous.

Elizabeth was ignoring her sister, looking for the policeman,
squinting and straining to see through the crowd. After a
moment or so, satisfied that he was not in pursuit, she turned to
look at Margaret. Emulsion-white, and livid with rage, she
snatched the helmet from her.

'How *could* you?' she snapped. 'How *could* you do such a
stupid, irresponsible thing?'

In any other situation, the men would have felt it their job to
intervene, and calm the ladies' bad temper, perhaps with a
supercilious hand on the arm. Such presumption was of course
out of the question here. They were silent.

'Oh, Lilibet, *come* on.'
'I will not come on.'
'*Come* on.'
'I will not.'
'Give me the helmet back.'
'Shan't.'
'At least wear it yourself.'
'Won't.'
'Or let Hugh wear it.'
'No.'

Margaret paused for a second, then attempted to grab the helmet back by force, and the sisters grappled and tussled almost to the ground as Hugh and Peter looked on. There was wolf-whistling from onlookers. Only the knowledge that they were making a spectacle of themselves ended the struggle, with Elizabeth still in possession. Sweaty, dishevelled, but careful to put their mock glasses back on, the women straightened and stared at each other defiantly.

'Margo,' said Elizabeth levelly, 'we are going together to take this helmet back to the policeman; you are going to return it and apologise.'

'Shan't.'
'Yes, you are.'
'No, I'm not.
'You jolly well will.'
'Jolly well won't.'
'Come along.'
'No.'
'Then I shall go myself.'

Elizabeth gave Margaret a moment to relent, but she was unrepentant. So she began to march back in the direction in which they had been running, cupping the helmet in both hands. Peter spoke up.

'Your Royal Highness.'

Instantly, all three – Elizabeth now from afar – turned around and quelled him with a fierce glance. He would give the game away. Apologetically, Peter approached her, and the others followed.

'I'm awfully sorry,' he murmured, 'but giving the helmet back might just tip them off as to who you are. Other people might find out, too. Or he might *not* realise who you are and just cut up frightfully rough and try to arrest you or something.'

'Yes, exactly!' piped up Margaret.

'Don't try to pretend you'd thought of all that.'

'I had.'

'You hadn't.'

'I had.'

'Oh, rot.'

Elizabeth walked slowly back. She knew they were right. It was a novel experience, having to argue, out here, in this crowded, democratic arena.

'All right,' she said, with as much good grace as she could muster, and handed the helmet back to Margaret. For an awful moment, all four thought that this quarrel would spoil the whole evening.

'I say, Your Royal Highness,' said Hugh quietly. 'Why not try the thing on yourself?'

'Oh yes, *do!*' said Margaret, magnanimous in victory, and once again returned it.

Elizabeth shrugged and smiled, perennially aware of the overwhelming importance, on this and every other occasion, of being a good sport. She put the helmet on. Everyone laughed supportively. She puffed out her cheeks and put on the same pop-eyed expression and wagged her finger. She did the voice.

''Ello, 'ello, 'ello. Now then, now then. What's all this? Let's be 'avin' you.'

They laughed, and so did a couple of young men in uniform, who cheerfully applauded. As if prompting her, they hummed some Gilbert and Sullivan, and before she knew quite what she was doing, Elizabeth shyly sang:

When a felon's not engaged in his employment ...

And her companions sang:

(His employment ...)

Or maturin' his felonious little plans ...
(Little plans ...)

His capacity for innocent enjoyment
(... cent enjoyment ...)

Is just as great as any honest man's!

By now a rather large crowd had sprung up, who all sang:

Whoooaaaaa ...
When constabulary duty's to be done, to be done, a policeman's lot
is not an 'appy one ...

Elizabeth had been conducting with two forefingers and, with a knee-bend, gamely contributed the final bass drone:

'Appy one ...

Everyone cheered and clapped, and Margaret kissed her sister on the cheek. Hurrah! Hurrah, hurrah, hurrah! The crowd melted away, in search of other entertainments, but Elizabeth continued to beam, as the significance of what had just happened dawned on her. She had just done something, which ... well, she had *done* something. Something which people liked. Done it herself. Nobody was sucking up to her; nobody was bowing the knee; nobody was pretending because nobody knew who she was. She'd done it! On her own!

Well, not exactly on her own. She went up to Margaret and whispered, 'I'm awfully sorry for being a bore!'

Chapter Four

'Likewise.'

'Pax?'

'Rather.'

They linked arms again and began to walk; the men fell in behind. A rather more traditional power relation had been established. For the first time, Elizabeth began to look at the people around her; freed from the need to make conversation, or wave, or defer, or gracefully accept deference, she started to look – and what she saw was kissing. People kissing. Everywhere. Margaret nudged her and pointed, discreetly, and Elizabeth nudged her back. They giggled. Margaret peeped behind to see if Hugh and Peter were reacting to this spectacle, but they maintained decorous, non-committal smiles. Mindful at all times of her responsibilities, she turned to bring Hugh into the conversation.

'Are all these people *married*, d'you suppose? Or engaged?' she asked him.

'Oh, of course, Your Royal Highness. Just not to each other.'

Hugh's sally got a gratifying, scandalised squeal from Margaret and an indulgent laugh from Elizabeth.

A little boy, lost, wandered into their path, blubbering and looking frantically round.

'Dad? Dad! Where are you, Dad?'

Elizabeth instantly went down on one knee with a concerned frown, but before she could ask him anything, a man appeared out of nowhere, grasped the child under the armpits, put him on his shoulders and capered away. Elizabeth couldn't see how the boy reacted; she couldn't be sure if this man actually was the father or not.

The unmistakable sound of a slapped face came from behind them.

'There's no need for that.'

'Well. Sauce.'

'You know what we agreed.'

'I agreed to no such thing.'

'Thief!'

The four of them whirled around again, to see two boys, one with a handbag under his arm running at full tilt in the direction of the Mall. A woman was giving ineffective chase, hobbled by heels which would have made even walking difficult. Her beau, clearly incapable with drink, was merely waving his fist.

'Oh lor,' commented Peter, weakly.

'Oh dear,' agreed Hugh.

'One hopes that this sort of thing is not going to be a feature of the evening.'

The crowd now became agitated at something. The mass rippled and parted. A figure was approaching; his presence was apparently not welcome, judging from the frowns, jeers and cat-calls. Someone started humming Gilbert and Sullivan again. It was their policeman, minus his helmet, walking quickly and purposefully in their direction.

'Corks!' said Margaret quaintly, and then, for the second time, 'Run!'

Five

Mr Ware grinned. He had just thrown a firework, a penny banger, into a shopfront doorway and it had made an almighty loud noise. Everyone had jumped, especially the two swell chaps in Guards uniforms he'd seen coming out of The Captain's Cabin. They had stared at him; he had stared back and someone shouted 'That's got the festivities started' and there was a huge laugh.

The evening was back the way he wanted it. Mr Ware was grateful for the laugh. He liked a bit of a pat on the back, metaphorical or otherwise. He'd actually had the most awful row with his wife before he'd left the flat – about their plans for the evening, and how exactly they were to get what he had decided they both wanted. There were rich pickings to be had, he told her. She said it was too dangerous. Too dangerous! As if they hadn't done dangerous things before now, and had dangerous things done to them!

At that moment, a very intoxicated Canadian in uniform literally attempted to pat him on the back, and Mr Ware instinctively pretended to be drunk too, slumping against him with a grin; he allowed himself to be helped up, while the man's girlfriends looked on, chattering and laughing.

'Y'okay?' the man laughed.

'Oh, yes, sorry, sorry, thanks very much!'

'B'bye now!'

'Cheer-o!'

The Canadian sauntered away, a lady friend on each arm if you please, and Mr Ware ducked round the corner, removed the Canadian's wallet from his inside jacket pocket and began to extract the cash. Ten pounds and ten shillings! And a French letter. He put the money and the rest of the doings down into his trouser pocket. The wallet went flapping down into a dustbin, like a dead bird.

You see? Windows of opportunity had to be scrambled through. Chances had to be grasped. But Mrs Ware, that shiftless and ungrateful slattern, did not see. She did not appreciate that this night offered them a real chance. Their final chance. Tomorrow the party would be over, and it would be back to peacetime civvy street.

Well, they had agreed in the end. That is, he had told Mrs Ware she would get another fourpenny one if she gave him gip. Last time that happened was when she had made a fuss about him carrying on at the Club. She didn't half get one that night, but she'd been provoking and provoking, for all the world as if she wanted one. She got one that night, all right. Actually, it was more like a sixpenny one. Just occasionally she'd got a ninepenny one, and on one occasion the full shilling. Whump.

Mr Ware felt for the bump in his belt, under his jacket, to check that what he'd stuffed down there was still in place. It was.

After meandering aimlessly about for an hour or so, Mr Ware wheeled north, skipping off the pavement into the thronged street itself, where the crush of people was lighter. He walked up Lower Regent Street in the direction of Piccadilly Circus. On the corner, a man was doing Find The Lady on an upturned cardboard box. Mr Ware recognised him, and exchanged a wink. The man threw a Queen, an Ace and another Ace face down on the cardboard surface; the cards often overlapped. A crowd of people, all male, from old men to boys, had gathered. One relatively well-dressed man had evidently been enticed to the front, and Mr Ware guessed that he would be the one of whom the card-player had great hopes. He wondered how many of the crowd were not stooges, and thought not many.

'No money, no money, no money, just for fun, which d'you think?' said the card-master, throwing the cards down once again.

Bashfully, the well-dressed man pointed to the card in the

middle and it was turned up. The Queen. There was an instant ragged cheer – part of the purpose of this part of the trick, apart from lulling the mark into a false sense of security, was to attract a bigger crowd.

'Ooh, you're good at this, come on, how about making it interesting? What about a ha'penny?'

To show he was a good sport, the man bet a halfpenny, and was successful again. There was another massive cheer, and the card-master, with a pantomime pout of astonishment at his customer's extraordinary, untrained skill at Finding The Lady, gave the man a penny and challenged him to have a real bet.

'Go on! Be a sport! You can't quit now! Give the poor feller a chance, sir,' said the crowd who were bustling in behind him, physically preventing him from leaving. In the distance, someone was singing 'I've got a luverly bunch of coconuts.'

'Come on. A quid.'

Intimidated, the man agreed to bet a pound. He swayed somewhat, and Mr Ware made a mental bet of his own – that the man had not been drinking at all, but felt constrained to explain away to the crowd and to himself the imminent disaster on the grounds that he was drunk. He betted a pound, pointed to one of the cards and of course on this occasion it was an Ace.

'Come on! Have another go! Get your money back.'

'No, no.' The man, thoroughly ashamed, tried to leave, was jostled back, and when he persisted, was jostled on his way by the spiteful, vengeful mob.

'G'wan then. On your way.' Instinctively, simply to partake of the fun, Mr Ware came forward and joined in the shoving of this unfortunate man, whose VE Night had now been entirely spoiled. An apprentice draughtsman, who lived in Ipswich and was up in the capital just for the evening, he went back to Ipswich on the early train the next morning and never came to London ever again.

Turning up into Great Windmill Street, Mr Ware found what he was looking for: the Butterfly Club. There was no sign or outward indication of any sort to the passer-by. To gain admission, Mr Ware had to crouch down on his haunches and reach awkwardly through a row of rusty railings that ran alongside a tobacconist's door and rap with his knuckle on a pane of glass. Presently, a figure appeared down there, looking up expressionlessly at Mr Ware, and then vanished. Then a cellar door opened and this man walked up a shallow flight of rusty metal steps, and unbolted a square section of mesh wire to allow access. Mr Ware followed him down through the door, and entered the premises. As he did so, through force of habit, he removed his wedding ring with some effort, and placed it in his pocket.

It was a surprisingly large room in an L-shape, with a bar on one side, tables and chairs; Mr Ware walked on to look around the corner where there was a small stage, a piano and a microphone on a stand. The stage was empty but not the bar, at which four or five men were standing, each wearing a boxy demob suit, smoking and without exception drinking gin. The one Mr Ware was looking for was quite obvious, from the way he flinched with alarm at the sight of him. It was Colin Erskine-Jones.

'Colin.'

Colin was actually sitting on a high stool which he now attempted to scramble off, perhaps to greet Mr Ware, perhaps to go to the lavatory, or perhaps to make a panicky escape. Mr Ware placed himself squarely against Colin, preventing him from moving. Colin rearranged his features in such a way as to suggest he was pleased to see him.

'My dear chap. My dear chap. Drink?'

'I was going to order a gin and It, Colin.'

'Do please let me get it,' quavered Colin, as if there was any question of anything else. 'What are you having? Oh yes, gin and It.'

Mr Ware nodded coolly and Colin made the order. Their drinks arrived. Colin offered Mr Ware a cigarette; this he took without a word of thanks, but rather as if it were a peace offering, which he would accept in an opaque spirit of diplomacy, without being in any way deflected from his main purpose.

'Now, Colin,' said Mr Ware, crushing his cigarette wastefully in the ashtray after one single puff. 'Do you have that money you owe me?'

'What money?' asked Colin in a quiet voice. The other men at the bar began to move away, to the tables, or to the exit.

'Half of what you got from selling the doings, Colin, the doings which I allowed you to procure from Bruton Street. That was a goldmine, Bruton Street, wasn't it? You must admit that.'

'Not quite as good as all that, old chap ...'

'I think there must have been some *earrings* Colin, in fact I think you're wearing one of them now ...'

With a circular swipe of his right hand, Mr Ware brought in the nails of his forefinger and thumb and pincered Colin's left earlobe with them, pulling the side of his head down towards the bar. The barman turned his back and busied himself washing out a glass.

'Ah-ah-ah-ah,' said Colin, suppressing his pain and fear, and trying to make this the kind of 'steady on' reproach one might use with a wayward child or puppy.

'*Wearing* them ...'

'Ah ...'

'Oh no! My mistake. You're not.'

He released Colin's now red-hot ear.

'Just my mistake. Whoops! Ha! Just my joke.' Mr Ware now considered it expedient to clown around a little. 'Just my joke, Colin, you're all right. Another gin? Another gin!'

They got more drinks, and this time the cigarettes were on Mr Ware. Resentful and emboldened, Colin now ventured a note of complaint. 'There really wasn't that much there, you know. Nothing much. Really nothing. Furniture's no bloody use at all.'

'Well, how about the cigarette case?'

'Tried selling that to a chap earlier today. Nothing doing. I say, are you *sure* it's solid silver? Shouldn't it have a hallmark? Mightn't it be just plate?'

But Mr Ware was now distracted by another matter entirely. A large woman with fierce blonde hair had come up behind him with an exaggerated hip-rolling gait, knees slightly bent. She gave Colin a wink and then playfully pounced on Mr Ware, putting claw-like hands over his eyes, and then whisked him round. From his wide, immediate grin, it was clear that Mr Ware did not at all mind this assault. He knew who this was from the beginning.

'Darling!' she croaked.

'My own one!' he replied smoothly, placing his cigarette in the ashtray.

The woman took Mr Ware's head in both hands and placed his face in her cleavage. To Colin, it seemed as though he was there for quite some time, making tiny mewing sounds. Some of the customers who had nervously left the bar a few minutes ago were beginning to return, to make fresh orders and stay at the bar.

At last, Mr Ware was freed. He wore the expression of a man who had been gazing at a sunset until the moment of nightfall.

'How are you, dearest?'

'Oh, I'm all right, you know,' he said, with a kind of post-coital tenderness.

The woman looked over at Colin. 'I look forward to seeing your act tonight, ducks,' she said, and added, 'Tonight is special.'

'It is special.' Both men agreed.

'It's a wonderful moment in our history,' she said. 'And Christ, loves, what a blessed relief not to have rationing any more.'

They both nodded.

'Mind you. We have to think about our boys out in the Far East. The job isn't over yet,' she said sternly. 'Out there, our boys battle on. We must never forget that. Never.'

They nodded again, and Colin was slightly relieved that there was someone of whom Mr Ware might be very slightly afraid.

'When I think about the Japanese ...' said Ginnie, her voice quietening and decelerating. There was a moment's quiet.

Chapter Five

'Anyway,' said Mr Ware, 'we're all really looking forward to the party tonight.'

'Jolly good!'

'And talking of which,' said Mr Ware, 'I wonder if young Colin and I could be permitted to pop behind the bar, down the stairs, and have a look at the various important things we have stored there?'

'Oh yes, oh yes, my dear,' said Ginnie genially. 'You bowl along. We have to make sure everything's present and correct, don't we?'

Ray, behind the bar, opened up the flap and Mr Ware motioned for Colin to come through and then lead the way round past the wall of drinks and spirit measures, and through a door at the other side. This passageway was very dark, lit only by a glimmer of light from an office at the far end. Colin knew the way; so did Mr Ware. There was no reason for them not to walk two abreast down this passageway and make conversation while they did so. But somehow Colin was made to walk ahead with Mr Ware behind, as if under arrest.

Turning right, Colin and Mr Ware found another door, which could only be fully opened after shoving and kicking some obstructions on the floor out of the way, and Colin reached around and turned on a light switch.

It was a storeroom. There were boxes, and files of discarded paperwork. These had to be heaved out of the way by Colin.

Presently, the men found what they were looking for: a dusty old hanger-rail, running on castors at either end, of the sort that you might find in a dry cleaner's, or a tailor's, or anyone in the rag trade. It had two coat-hangers, of which one had a set of blue overalls, and an ARP helmet hanging by its chinstrap: white with a single diamond. Mr Ware took his uniform down, rolled it up, and thoughtfully put it in a bag. He wasn't sure exactly when he was going to need this.

The other hanger held something longer and fuller, something concealed under a paper cover which was intended to protect it from dust. It was Colin who peeled this back to check that everything was all right under there.

'Your gown, madame?' said Mr Ware.

'Yes,' said Colin quietly. Something about this rich and exotic garment restored some of Colin's confidence, and in fact Mr Ware became more respectful as well, standing back.

'Everything ship-shape about it?' he asked.

'Oh, perfectly.'

'I had it taken in, just as you asked.'

'Thank you.'

'Not that you needed it. It's not as if you've gained weight.'

'Well,' said Colin judiciously, with a you-can't-be-too-careful tone.

'Did you want to try it on?' asked Mr Ware, now almost humble.

'No,' said Colin, 'that's all right. We'll wait until later.'

'Right-o.'

'I suppose I could sketch out some of the dance steps.'

Forty-five minutes later, both men reappeared in the bar, dusty and subdued. Ginnie beamed over at them; she was now helping out with the serving of drinks. The place was a bit more crowded.

'Everything all right?' she called out.

Mr Ware did not reply. His sour mood had evidently returned. It was for Colin to say that, yes, yes, everything was present and correct. Mr Ware had his ARP bundle under his arm. Colin's earlobe still throbbed red.

'I suppose you chaps know Rupert?'

They saw a handsome, younger man sitting at the bar, a double whisky in front of him. He looked up and smiled coolly. They had not been introduced.

'This is Rupert,' said Ginnie, unconsciously patting the back of her hair, pushing it springily into the scalp behind both ears in turn. 'He's one of my most loyal customers in the Brown Bomber.' This was Ginnie's other Soho club.

Rupert stood up and put out his hand to Mr Ware to shake, and then to Colin.

'Delighted,' he said. 'Brook. Rupert Brook.'

54

'With – *out* the 'e', chaps,' said Ginnie. 'And Rupert is being too modest. He's not in uniform tonight, but he is in fact Group Captain Rupert Brook. Of the RAF.'

Rupert smiled tolerantly, as if he really couldn't approve of Ginnie's extravagant praise.

'The Few,' said Ginnie reverently. 'One of The Few.'

Brook was a handsome man with a fleshy, placid face, which appeared to crease easily into a beaming smile – as it did now. He wore a chalkstripe suit whose shoulders were dusted with dandruff; his tie bore some crest or other.

'Ginnie,' he said, in a voice slower and more languid than the others', 'I was wondering if I couldn't possibly get something to eat from that kitchen of yours?'

'Right you are, Group Captain!'

Brook made a small *moue* of exasperation at her flattery.

'And perhaps these gentlemen would like to join me in some snack or other ...?' he ventured.

'I could do you all a jolly filling sausage sandwich each.'

'Marvellous. Does that sound up to the mark, chaps?' he asked.

Colin thanked him heartily, but Mr Ware, though unwilling to pass the offer up, was reluctant to put himself in this man's debt.

'Now, remind me,' said Group Captain Brook, 'what is it you do, again?'

'I am – I was – an ARP warden,' said Mr Ware stoutly.

'Ah, yes. But in civilian life?'

'I was a builder.'

'Ah. Jolly good. And what about you, Colin?'

'I'm in the wine trade. Was before the War, anyway. Now I really don't know.'

'Well, Ginnie tells me that you have theatrical interests. I expect they'll be keeping you busy, won't they?'

'Oh yes.'

Presently, their sausage sandwiches arrived and all three men started chomping away. Group Captain Brook did not remove his jacket, but contrived to keep his sleeves entirely free of grease.

'I myself had interests in a couple of West End shows in '38. They did remarkably well. I turned a pretty penny without lifting a finger. And people want entertainment now more than ever. There's a nice little theatrical pie I've got my finger into now, actually. Of course, there's room for investors of the right sort.'

Brook let that remark hang in the air. Mr Ware was too suspicious to follow it up, and Colin Erskine-Jones too gloomy and too poor.

'Well, cheer-o,' said Brook, lifting his whisky, draining it, and then with a tap of his finger on the glass, followed by a circular teaspoon-stirring movement in the air, indicated that he would like another and intended to buy the others theirs as well. A raised eyebrow in their direction solicited the information that they would like whiskies. Brook mouthed the word 'whiskies' in the direction of the bar.

'Jolly good work you're doing in the ARP, Ware,' Brook now said thoughtfully. 'Jolly *hard* work, too, come to that.'

'Well, it was difficult work, but somebody had to do it,' said Ware. Colin remained silent, although Ware's observation could as well have applied to him.

'Really thankless stuff,' continued Brook, as if the subject was so extraordinary, so riveting, he simply couldn't leave it alone. 'Badly paid. Unpaid, actually. And of course as there are still bombsites and unsafe areas ...?'

Mr Ware's eyes, as he now looked at Group Captain Brook, had the shuttered, opaque quality of a guard dog at heel. He was silent in a way that made Colin squirm with discomfiture, but Brook remained entirely open, candid and cheerful.

'Ginnie's been telling me all about the hard work you've been doing – and the *risks* you've been taking.'

Both Ware and Colin, entirely independently, turned around to see where Ginnie was. But she had evidently disappeared.

'Because it's a risky business. Unlike my business. Did Ginnie tell you what my business is?'

Mr Ware turned back to Brook and neither nodded nor shook his head.

'It's antiques. Furniture. And jewellery,' Brook prattled on. 'I deal with all sorts of valuables. Large and small. Commonplace and rare. I buy and I sell. And I can act as an agent. I can handle a lot of material and I can place it with buyers who are not burdened with – how shall I say? – a neurotic insistence on knowing the provenance of each piece. Do you understand what I mean?'

Ginnie chose this moment to reappear with the whiskies. She set the tray down, and just as Group Captain Brook was reaching into his pocket, Mr Ware forestalled him with a downward-palm gesture, and produced a ten-shilling note himself. He was smiling.

Six

Running had been, on this second occasion, easier but less fun; the novelty had dwindled and Elizabeth had been relieved when they all decided they had eluded the pursuer, who was probably not in the slightest bit serious about the chase. The four were now much further up, in the crowds near Trafalgar Square.

In her heart, Elizabeth considered that it was high time they returned to the Palace. This had, surely, been quite enough. She was secretly amazed at the extraordinary things that they had done – that she had done! Not only stealing a policeman's helmet – well, Margaret had done that – but wearing it and leading an impromptu sing-song. Incredible! Elizabeth was almost overcome with euphoria thinking about this wonderful *coup*, but knew that it would not entirely overwhelm her until she was back inside, safe, chattering about it with her sister, with Bobo, even with her father!

There were two people that she knew she couldn't regale with these stories. One was the Queen who, although by no means humourless, could never countenance these shenanigans. The other was Philip. With absolute clarity, Elizabeth foresaw in detail the puzzlement and irritated resentment with which he would react. A piece of mannish daring and high-jinks in which he had not been present – which, indeed, could never have happened had he been present? Oh dear, no. He would not laugh and clap his hands delightedly, as Elizabeth imagined the King doing. On the contrary. He would be furious. It might well colour the vital first months of their married life together. And this was not even taking into account the presence of two unmarried young Guards officers, squiring the Princesses around. There was of course no question of impropriety, but shrewdly, anxiously, Elizabeth assessed this as a matter of status and *amour propre*. She wondered if Philip would take offence, and refuse to forgive these two officers for giving his fiancée such an unforgettable night on the tiles. Should she refuse to give their names, if he pressed her? Should she claim that she and Margaret had been out on their own? Or with other people entirely?

No. That wouldn't do. The only thing was simply not to tell him at all. But wouldn't he find out from the King?

'Do come along, Lilibet,' said Margaret. 'What shall we do now? I say, shall we go for a drink somewhere?'

Elizabeth knew that this insouciant pose, this casual talk of going for a drink, was all nonsense. Margaret had of course never gone for a drink anywhere in her life. She had only this Christmas been permitted wine. Elizabeth herself did not like the taste, all that much.

Suddenly, from nowhere, Elizabeth conceived an overwhelming irritation with Margaret and these two gallants who were dancing attendance on her sister and making her feel excluded and unwanted; for a second, a profound and contemptuous uninterest in the two men's lives swept over her and she wished all three would just go anywhere, go away.

'We might go to the Ritz, Your Royal Highness,' murmured Hugh. He was talking to Margaret.

'Oh, do let's!' said Margaret.

The three of them turned questioningly to Elizabeth, and she was wasp-stung with irritation to realise that they were not asking for her opinion, but merely her permission.

'It really is getting awfully crowded,' Hugh presumed to add, as if to hurry her.

It was. The crowd, though still entirely cheerful, was densely packed, and moving anywhere required turning sideways and presenting one's shoulder. Conversations had to be conducted at a shout. To Margaret's obvious exasperation, Elizabeth still did not say anything. Standing there was becoming uncomfortable. But then something happened which made their minds up for them. From a distance, she could a hear a crowd beginning to sing 'Knees Up Mother Brown', and the raucous song appeared to be taken up by people nearer and nearer to them. And the crowd seemed to be reforming, quite oddly, lining up like iron filings when a magnet is brought close. An old man quite near Elizabeth put his hands – rather lasciviously, Elizabeth thought – on the hips of a pretty young woman in front of him, and didn't appear to react when a middle-aged woman put her hands on his hips. They were singing 'Knees Up Mother Brown', too.

'A conga line!' squealed Margaret. 'Come on, Lilibet!'

Reluctantly, Elizabeth placed her hands very lightly on the hips of the young man in front who had joined this uproarious musical queue – or rather, higher, nearer the small of his back. Margaret put her hands on her hips. Glancing back, she noticed that Hugh had put his hands on Margaret's hips, and supposed that Peter had placed his hands on Hugh's. They started moving off, part of the long ungainly human snake that had started to jog towards Admiralty Arch, and was perhaps at this moment going round and round Nelson's Column.

> *If I catch you bending*
> *I'll saw your legs right off*
> *Knees up, knees up,*
> *Don't get the breeze up,*
> *Knees up, Mother Brown.*

As quickly as it had arisen, Elizabeth's silent bad temper vanished. Actually, this was fun! The dancing aspect of the whole thing was just a matter of rocking from side to side and kicking out one's feet occasionally. Much less demanding than the reels at Balmoral over Christmas, but just as vigorous. Under the table you will go!

When they reached the end of the song, everyone just seemed happy to go back to the beginning again. After a while, they changed to 'We'll Hang Out Our Washing on the Siegfried Line'.

Elizabeth was getting rather puffed, but was still perfectly happy. She looked ahead, and wondered if the conga line was going all the way up Whitehall. And behind her, did it stretch all the way down to the Palace and back to Victoria? Was there some fleeting, ecstatic moment in which everyone in London was connected up in one vast conga line? Black-cab drivers, after studying The Knowledge, were supposed to be vouchsafed a vision in which they could 'see it', see the entirety of London's streets in their heads, all at once. Elizabeth wondered if she was experiencing something similar.

It was odd, though, this conga line business. When *was* it going to end? And wasn't it strange not facing the person you were dancing with? That was what happened with normal dances. And with all other group things, such as a reel, or a Dashing White Sergeant, there were boundaries, conventions, regulations.

'Margo!' Elizabeth called experimentally over her shoulder, and then thought to disguise her voice. 'Margo!' she growled in an absurdly low Scottish accent, and giggled. It was a pointless precaution. Nobody could hear a word in this crush and din. So she turned around to talk to her.

But Margaret wasn't there. The person behind her was a plump, middle-aged woman, wearing a porridgey overcoat that bulged and split at three points down the front where she had done up the buttons. This woman winked and grinned at Elizabeth, who did her best to grin back, but then instantly turned round to face front, pale. Where on earth were Margaret, Hugh and Peter? And where was she now, anyway? Fortunately, the looming landmark of Admiralty Arch gave the answer to that question. But where on earth were the others? Elizabeth wondered if she dared turn around again or call out for them, and risk being recognised.

She turned around, and – converting her tense grimace into a grin – tried to examine the tapering train of bodies for signs of Margaret and the two men. They were not there. They were gone. She was alone.

Elizabeth did not at first realise that she was entirely at liberty to free herself from the conga line and look for them properly. But a lifetime of formal engagements had taught her that, in the event of a crisis, with all eyes being on her, the best thing was to keep going as if nothing was wrong. So she just went on, jogging and conga-ing, frantically wondering where they had got to.

Every other person seemed to be collapsing boozily on the ground. It was getting dark. Finally, Elizabeth extricated herself from the human snake and searched frantically, while keeping her bogus spectacles glued to her face with her finger and thumb.

'Margo. Margo.' Elizabeth didn't dare shout the words, so ridiculously said them at normal, and inaudible, talking volume. She became silent.

Well, it was too bad. Margaret had clearly tired of the whole thing and turned tail, heading for home. They might have told her. And the men might have had the gumption to stand up to Margaret in this caprice. Or perhaps leaving her alone like this was some sort of prank. Yes, that was it. Elizabeth's paleness was now due more to anger than fear. Well, there was nothing for it, but to walk back to the Palace, unaccompanied. And if Margaret and the others caught it, well, it was just jolly well their own fault.

Elizabeth set about stalking home, her euphoric mood now utterly cancelled. But this was not easy. The parks authority seemed to have put up barriers which blocked her advance at every turn, like a maze. And then there were the crowds, which were becoming ever more boisterous and drunken. Keeping her glasses held in place, Elizabeth now realised that getting recognised would be a calamity – though the dark disorder actually made it unlikely – and so she tried to walk while keeping her eyes fixed to the ground. Periodically, she would look up and see that she had been walking in the wrong direction entirely. And people would keep crashing and bumping into her.

Far over to her right, an unruly crowd was singing 'What Shall We Do with the Drunken Sailor?' and on the 'up she rises' line was actually throwing someone up into the air, tossed from a blanket or coat. Was it a woman or a man, a boy or a girl? He or she seemed to be crying 'stop' or 'help'. Elizabeth couldn't quite hear. She went up on tiptoe to see, couldn't, then went up on tiptoe again, and was knocked to the ground. A wave of bodies surged drunkenly from somewhere behind and to the right of her.

Elizabeth screamed. She locked her elbows into her ribcage, clenched her fists in such a way as to bring her tensed wrists to her cheeks, and brought her knees up, in an awful parody of the song. She thought she might be trampled half to death and many people stumbled over her, falling over themselves, and causing other people to fall over.

No one offered to help her up, and no one asked if she was all right. They just kept jumping and stumbling over her: a continuous Becher's Brook, scrambling and flailing overhead. Elizabeth was able to get herself up on her elbows, and had rescued her bogus spectacles, resettling them on her nose. She shuffled along the ground on elbows and knees, and found herself relatively in the clear, but when she tried to stand up, to her intense mortification and disgust, Elizabeth felt faint, and might easily have fallen back down again.

'I say, are you all right?'

There was a hand – actually, three or four fingertips – on her shoulder. Elizabeth looked up.

An alert, amused young woman was looking down at her. She was wearing an unflattering, closely fitting chocolate brown suit, sensible brown shoes, and – even in this first instant, Elizabeth could see this – rather too much makeup, which gave her kindly face a waxen look. Elizabeth did not reply at first, and nothing in her upbringing had schooled her in how to respond to an unsolicited remark from a member of the public who was addressing her on the assumption of equal terms.

'Are you all right?' the woman repeated, and then said, with

63

an indulgent chuckle, 'One over the eight, is it? Well, we're all at it, tonight!'

Elizabeth was now stung, and rapidly got up.

'I certainly am not drunk!' she said hotly.

Untroubled by her irritation, the woman continued in the same vein. She had perhaps heard the same declaration from drunks many times before.

'Oh, all right then, all right. Let's get you straightened out.' With the stiffened, flattened palm of her hand, the woman then brushed the dirt off Elizabeth's uniform; about the grass stains, she could do nothing.

'Is that everything?' she asked, squinting at the fabric in the gloom. 'I'm afraid I've gone and left my glasses at home, so I can't quite see.'

'Yes, I think that's everything,' said Elizabeth evenly. 'Thank you.'

Neither said anything for a moment, and although a gaggle of people near them were now doing a 'hands, knees, and boomps-a-daisy' dance that left them sprawled and giggling on the ground, while one of them twanged on a banjo, the dense centre of the crowd seemed to have passed elsewhere. It was relatively quiet.

'My name's Katharine, by the way.' Katharine stuck her hand directly out. Elizabeth shook it politely, wondering whether to give her real first name.

'And you are …?'

'Lil,' said Elizabeth, fudging the issue.

'Right-o. What do you think of all this, then?'

'Remarkable.'

'Where are you stationed?'

'Windsor. And you – civvy street, I suppose?'

'Rather. I work in St James's. Well, actually in Whitehall. I'm a secretary to – well, I shouldn't say.' Katharine looked a little flirtatious. 'I'm actually secretary to some highups. I really shouldn't say.'

It occurred to Elizabeth to have some mild sport with this woman and her 'highups'.

'Really?' she prompted, affecting wide-eyed admiration. 'Who? Who d'you mean?'

'Well, I work in *Downing Street*. And sometimes I take dictation from ...'

'Gosh,' said Elizabeth, 'you don't mean ...?'

'I do!' said Katharine. 'Mr *Morrison!* He's awfully nice.'

'Jolly good,' said Elizabeth, already feeling ashamed to have secretly mocked.

'I say,' Katharine then said, 'I'm awfully sorry for saying you were tight. It's absolutely plain that you aren't. Sorry about that.'

'Not a bit.'

They stood around for a moment. It was now almost entirely dark, though the throng was lit in pools from the street lights along the Mall. Elizabeth knew that she now ought to be making her way back to the Palace as quickly as possible, and yet years of training in graceful gratitude had taught her that simply leaving Katharine was not correct. She noticed a wedding ring on Katharine's left hand.

'Is your husband with you tonight?' she asked politely.

'Oh, he couldn't get away,' said Katharine breezily. 'He's always got a lot of work on.' Katharine looked for a ring on Elizabeth, too. 'I say, Lil, do you have a chap?'

'Oh yes,' said Elizabeth, 'I'm engaged to be married.'

Elizabeth realised that she had never actually spoken these words out loud to anyone before. Just saying them had a liberating, exhilarating effect. Instantly she felt better and smiled, and this produced a warm, wide smile from Katharine too.

'Well, you've got something else to celebrate tonight, haven't you?' Elizabeth nodded. She supposed that she had. It was all she could do to stop grinning from ear to ear like a madwoman. What was the *matter* with her? Had VE Night brought out some sort of instability? But even this thought, so far from sobering Elizabeth, tempted her to giggle further.

'Why don't we drink a toast to that?' said Katharine suddenly. She produced a green leather flask from a hip pocket, unscrewed the silver top and offered it to her.

Elizabeth took it, smiled a silent thanks, and swigged. From somewhere, she couldn't think where – the pictures? Cowboy films? – she knew that she was supposed to wipe her mouth and hand the flask back with a worldly grin. Drinking in the street! But she stood there, dumbly, holding the open flask. Katharine gently took it back from her. The liquid contents were … what were they, actually? Brandy? Whisky? Elizabeth had no idea. Anyway, the drink was branching through her veins, making her feel giddy and keen. Elizabeth was no Methodist. She had had wine before, and was reasonably sure she had tasted spirits too. But she couldn't remember them ever having this effect on her. She supposed it was the combined effect of the drink, the atmosphere, and having been knocked over. Or rather, having been rescued from having been knocked over. That was it.

'Do you think I could have another sip? Do you mind?'

'Not at all.'

Elizabeth now took a good swig. Katharine took the flask back from her and had one herself.

'Ha, take a pull on that – it's a bellrope!' said Elizabeth, remembering Arthur Askey on the wireless.

Katharine gave a polite though slightly mystified-sounding laugh.

'I say, if we walk over here a bit, we can get out of this crowd.'

They did so, Katharine swinging her arms easily. Elizabeth realised that she should be getting back to the Palace, and found herself wondering if they were worried about her. In the next instant, she thought: Oh blow. *Let* them worry.

They walked in silence. Katharine offered Elizabeth the flask and she took another drink.

'Lil,' asked Katharine, 'where's your chap now? What does he do?'

'He's in the Navy.'

'Ah. Jolly good,' said Katharine.

Elizabeth returned, 'How about yours?'

'He's in civvy street, back home.'

Something in the thought appeared to make Katharine

thoughtful and, simply to cover the silence, Elizabeth asked for yet another nip from the flask. That really would have to be her last.

'Oh, really!' Katharine seemed to have spotted something which caused her some amused exasperation. 'Look at that.'

Elizabeth looked, but couldn't see what she was supposed to be looking at.

'What?'

'Look. Courting couples.'

Elizabeth looked harder and then saw them. They were everywhere. Why hadn't she seen them before? It was like nudging the reception on a wireless dial which made everything loud and clear after a lot of growling and fizzing. Men and women kissing passionately in the gloom. Under trees. On the ground, on blankets which had rolled up over them. She could even see legs poking out from bushes. She could also see single women standing around on their own, smoking and looking about, as if waiting for someone. How odd.

'This is supposed to be VE Night. VD Night is more like it, if you ask me!'

Elizabeth did not have the smallest clue what Katharine was talking about. However, in her high good humour and out of politeness to her rescuer and new friend, she returned Katharine's knowing smile. Katharine sighed.

'When are you getting married, Lil?' she asked, suddenly.

'I'm – I'm really not sure,' said Elizabeth, surprised to add this to the many things that she did not know about her future.

'Will it be a church wedding?'

'Oh yes.'

'I only ask because some people don't. You know – have weddings in church.'

'Mine will be. Was yours?'

'What?'

'Was your wedding in a church?'

'Yes,' said Katharine vaguely. 'Yes it was. A jolly nice church. And we went to Margate for our honeymoon. Where are you going for your honeymoon?'

Again, Elizabeth was disconcerted to realise that she did not know, and could not be certain how much say she had in this matter, if indeed she had any at all.

'Well, I – I don't really know.'

Katharine gave Elizabeth a playful slap on the arm.

'Oh, Lil, don't be so feeble! You *must* know.'

'I don't, really I don't.'

'But you must have some idea?'

Elizabeth pulled herself together and tried to think of somewhere.

'Well, how about France?'

'The Riviera, you mean? The Cote D'Azur?'

Elizabeth tried imagining what these places were like, tried thinking of what the worldly thing to say about them might be.

'Well, yes, possibly,' she allowed, as if these choices were acceptable, but rather too obvious.

'Antibes? Juan Les Pins?'

'Mm,' said Elizabeth, 'I suppose.'

'Or what about Monte Carlo?'

'Yes, that could be an idea.'

'Oh, Lil, you are a tease!' Katharine burst out laughing, and slapped her arm again. Elizabeth looked puzzled once more.

'Monte Carlo! Juan Les Pins! As if any of us has the money for that sort of thing! What a leg-pull!'

Elizabeth attempted to join in the chortling, as if congratulating herself for pulling someone's leg. But hadn't it been Katharine who had suggested all those places? Their laughter, that is to say Katharine's laughter, died gently away and was replaced by another pensive quiet.

'Your honeymoon. Your wedding night. It's the most important night of your life.' Elizabeth could see that her friend's expression was very serious. 'It is when you know your husband for the first time.' Katharine turned to look at Elizabeth, sharply. 'I take it that this would be the case with you?'

'Oh yes,' Elizabeth nodded earnestly.

Looking mollified, Katharine returned the subject. 'For the

first time. The very first time. Between those sheets. A sacrament. You submit to him. It is the price.' Katharine laughed, to signal that this serious part of the conversation was over.

'Well,' she giggled. 'That's the wedding night. All bets are off. Don't you agree?'

Another absolutely inexplicable remark.

'Oh yes.'

'When my husband and I had our Margate honeymoon, we didn't emerge from our room for four days!'

'Had you had shellfish?' Elizabeth asked.

There was a great zoom and a whoosh. Celebratory Lancasters were flying overhead, absurdly low. Irresponsible, surely? But this was VE Night. Elizabeth suppressed an upsurge of fear and disapproval and replaced them with genial, tolerant bemusement. And in truth, she was in a very good mood.

'Oh goodness, it's at times like these that one feels lonely, doesn't one?' said Katharine, surveying the courting couples once more.

'Mm.'

'One has nobody to kiss oneself.'

'No.'

'When are you next going to see your chap, Lil?'

'Oh, I'm not sure.'

'One feels that one is jolly well in danger of getting out of practice!'

'Ha!'

'One shouldn't like to get out of practice.'

'Rather not.'

'Well, one jolly well isn't going to be left out of things. One wants to be in practice, after all.'

Before Elizabeth knew what was happening, Katharine moved around to stand in front of her and placed her hands on Elizabeth's shoulders, as if positioning her for a photograph. Then she placed her hands, gently but firmly as before, on Elizabeth's hips, leaned in and kissed her on the mouth. Elizabeth felt Katharine's forehead pressing against her spectacles; she could smell Katharine's pepperminty breath and the flicker of her tongue. She had a funny, fluttery feeling in her stomach. After a while, Katharine broke away, and keeping an arm around Elizabeth's waist she swung around to survey the scene once more.

'Ah, Lil,' she said dreamily, somehow addressing both her and those heedless couples that Elizabeth could now see everywhere. 'What a night! What a pity neither of us has got anyone to kiss. But there we are. One has to bear up. Ours is not to reason why, and so on. Don't you think?'

'Yes.'

'Well, there's no point in hanging around here. The time is getting on. Let's go and get a proper drink. What do you say?'

'Well, I don't know.'

'Oh, go on,' said Katharine, pushing out her lower lip in a pouty expression. 'Be a pal.'

Seven

What shall we do with the drunken sailor?
What shall we do with the drunken sailor?
What shall we do with the drunken sailor – early in the morning?

Ooo-ay and UP she rises!

Peter felt his body touch the ground, hard enough for his spine to
be jarred on a discarded tin can, before the crowd, holding the
tarpaulin on which he was being tossed, wrenched it taut and
hoisted it again so that he was hurled upwards. At ground level,
he was able to glimpse Hugh's smile, amused and alarmed in a
ratio of three to one, and Margaret's fixed smirk.

They had only been part of the conga line for a minute or so
before the Princess had become very bored, and then fascinated by
a crowd of men nearby who were throwing people up in the air,
really quite high, in what looked like some sort of cloth or blanket.

'Oooh, look!' she had shouted. 'I want to have a turn!' She
detached herself from the line and so, quickly, did her two
protectors, each assuming the other was keeping an eye on
Elizabeth.

'Oh, let's have a go!' she had called to them, her eyes
unnaturally bright with mischief and excitement. 'Oh, do let's!'

She ran over and started talking to one of the men, who was
just letting someone free from the tossing: a middle-aged
woman, slightly tearful but forcing herself to laugh
good-naturedly, revealing that the thing was much more of an
ordeal than she had anticipated. Margaret was showing every
sign of wanting to be next.

'Your Royal—' said Hugh urgently, and corrected himself,

'Your Roy— You real— You really shouldn't do this, please. I'm sorry—' Hugh made a bland, ingratiatingly good-sport gesture to the crowd, who were inching closer. 'I'm sorry, we really have to get on. *Please.*'

Margaret turned to him, highly displeased. She put her hands on her hips and glanced past him – perhaps taking in, as Hugh now realised, Elizabeth's continued attachment to the conga line. How *would* they re-insert themselves into that conga line, come to think of it?

There were cries of 'Come on' and 'Be a sport' from the men, all in civilian clothes. Some had shirts off; they had tied them around their waists like schoolboys, standing there in their vests, and with a tiny, fastidious shudder, Hugh registered the prominence of their chest and armpit hair.

'I think it looks fun,' said Margaret, her face now set. 'I think it would be very jolly.'

Both Hugh and Peter felt their faces contract and pulse with competing needs: to deny the Princess this unwise request, and a need to placate her, to placate the crowd and to withhold from the crowd the Princess's identity.

'Should we not, um, *rejoin the conga line?*' The fatuity of this last remark from Peter went fortunately unnoticed, being timidly inaudible.

One of the men belched, another laughed, and a third stretched, put his palms behind his head and flexed his upper arms, revealing symmetrical tattoos of birds. Peter and Hugh could see Margaret changing her mind.

'I don't mean me doing it,' she then said, crisply. 'I mean one of you doing it.'

'Well now,' began Peter, in the sad, worldly tone of one forced by circumstance to deny a reasonable request.

'Oh, all right then, Peter!' interrupted Hugh genially, gesturing to him with an open palm, and both he and the Princess stood back, to give Peter a clear path to the tarpaulin, which was being picked up again by the men who shuffled around and pulled it into a roughly circular shape, like firemen preparing to catch someone jumping from a burning building. It was apparently a groundsheet.

'Come on, mate!'

'Come on, if you're coming!'

'Come *on!*'

The men, Hugh and the Princess herself had instantly assumed the manner of people who were granting Peter's request, though a little impatient at his puppyish immaturity.

Peter felt his face sag, though it snapped into a fleeting grimace of resentment at Hugh as he walked past him – Hugh met it with a bland smirk – and then into the good-sport grin he knew was expected of him. Everyone in the vicinity persisted in behaving as if they were indulging his whim.

Peter climbed onto the taut material, wondering if he should take his shoes off. He expected a ragged, supportive cheer. Disconcertingly, there was a sudden, weird quiet. To initiate the proceedings, Margaret began to sing:

Ooo-ay and UP he rises!

They started to throw Peter into the air, and instead of a rhythmic, invigorating trampoline bounce, Peter experienced a series of brutal wrenches. As he was flung skywards, he felt the blood rush unpleasantly into his head; only after two or three times did he think to close his eyes.

'Wait!' he shouted, or perhaps it was 'Stop!' or 'Help!'

The fun continued.

After half a dozen throws, Peter opened his eyes and caught a glimpse of faces, grinning faces, jeering faces, blank faces, that all suddenly turned upwards.

There was a massive roar overhead. Peter thought that something had exploded, or that the Germans had finally achieved a last-gasp success with a new, undreamt-of secret weapon. But no, it was some sort of fly-past, a salute from RAF aircraft whose pilots on any other day would have been subject to court martial. Were they Lancasters?

The entire crowd gasped and cheered; the men all let go of the tarpaulin as Peter was on his eighth and final descent. He landed, very hard, on his left shoulder and elbow, and felt the tin can's sharp edge under his back.

'Hooray!' cheered the crowd.

'Argh,' said Peter, whose arm was broken.

'Wha-hay!' shouted the crowd.

'Ow, I, ah …' said Peter. His face was the colour of chalk.

Zoom, went the Lancasters as they headed off.

'Well, jolly good,' said Margaret. 'Where's Lilibet?'

'Your Royal Highness,' said Peter, for whom pain had extinguished the need to keep secrets, 'I can't move my arm.'

'Where's Lilibet?'

'I think my arm is broken.'

'Your Highness,' said Hugh.

'Lilibet? Lilibet! Where is Lilibet?'

'Your Highness?'

'Where are you, Lilibet?'

'Your Highness?'

'I can't see her anywhere. Where is the conga line?'

'She might be further ahead, towards Trafalgar Square.'

'Lilibet! Lilibet!'

'My arm.'

'Oh my God.'

'Lilibet!'

'Uh.'

Hugh and Margaret stood motionless and wordless, as the crowd swelled away from them. Peter was still left on the neglected tarpaulin, like a castaway on a raft. He was drifting in and out of consciousness. Margaret ran some way across the littered grass, looking for Elizabeth, and then back to where Hugh was standing, also scanning the crowd. Then she trotted in the opposite direction, looking, and ran back. She was always hopeless at finding things.

'Uh.' Peter returned to a bleary wakefulness. Margaret looked over to him, pity and concern in her face entirely subordinate to

74

irritation and distaste. Peter tried to speak to her, and vomited weakly down his chin. Someone nearby said something about not holding his drink.

Hugh bent over Peter and listened as he whispered that he could not move his arm. Then Hugh quickly removed his jacket and attempted to make a rudimentary sling from his shirt, all the time frantically and pointlessly looking around for signs of Elizabeth.

'I think *that's* her!' said Margaret, and ran off to a young woman standing in shadow under a tree. Hugh and Peter limped and straggled behind as Margaret shouted, 'Lilibet, Lilibet,' now entirely heedless of the need to remain incognito.

The woman turned to them, her face in shadow. It was only then that all three of them saw that she was not in uniform, but in some sort of dark coat and skirt, and that she was smoking a cigarette, her right elbow cupped in her left palm.

'Five shillings each,' was all she said.

'I do beg your pardon,' said Hugh, as Margaret turned away and Peter vomited once again.

Singing and rowdiness and cigarette smoke drifted in the wind as night fell further. The trio mentally exerted themselves to the utmost to suppress their fear.

'Well, we appear to have become split up from Her Royal Highness, in the crowds,' said Hugh at last, a great believer in exerting mastery over any situation by speaking and summarising, however superfluous his words would appear. Peter groaned, and Hugh grunted as he shifted his own weight to keep Peter upright.

Margaret herself was speechless, and in a state of some suspense, postponing her vituperation and scorn for when this situation was rectified by her attendants.

Hugh cleared his throat with a bark and then said, 'What Her Royal Highness has undoubtedly done ... what she has undoubtedly done is set off back to the Palace on her own.'

'I've broken my arm.'

Both Hugh and Margaret ignored Peter as the reality of this situation dawned on them. Elizabeth would present herself at the side gate of the Palace again, present her warrant card, and be re-admitted. There would then be the most ferocious row, especially if she had to encounter Their Majesties on her own. The fuss would be bad enough for Elizabeth and then for Margaret, but for Peter and Hugh it would indeed be horrible.

'My arm.'

But surely, Hugh pondered, Elizabeth herself would sense all of this, and be very reluctant simply to head off back to the Palace? They had, after all, only been separated for half an hour. They should look for her.

Peter almost fainted again, and Hugh clutched him.

'I say,' said Margaret loudly, to three young women in nurses' uniforms that were walking past nearby.

'Yes?' one replied.

'This man would appear to be in some pain. We think he has broken his arm.' Margaret left it ambiguous as to whether or not she was actually acquainted with the injured party.

'Oh?'

'Do you happen to know if there's anywhere he can go?'

'Yes,' said a second nurse eagerly. 'There's a medical station in Charing Cross – St John's Ambulance.'

'Oh jolly good. *Would* you mind taking this poor man there?' said Margaret, adroitly implying that in volunteering this information, they had also volunteered to accompany Peter to Charing Cross. Helpfully, and piteously, Peter then fell forwards in the women's direction. The second and third women bent down to pick him up while the first continued to look keenly at Margaret's face.

'Thanks awfully,' said Hugh, instinctively interposing himself between the two women and preventing recognition. 'That's awfully good of you. I think he can walk. You can walk, can't you, old chap?'

Peter straightened up and was able to stagger alongside the nurses, his arms around their shoulders, without having to be a deadweight. He was now pale and silent, and hardly responded to his fellows' hearty farewell. The four of them disappeared.

Hugh turned around and to his dismay found that Margaret was now smoking a cigarette – having presumably secreted the packet about her person – and was again looking around the throng, that sweet oval face expressionless.

'Your Royal Highness,' said Hugh urgently, 'what I suggest we do is this. Let us walk up to Trafalgar Square together. Then I think we should split up. I shall search up St Martin's Lane. You walk up Pall Mall, and into the Haymarket and back, and we can rendezvous back at, let's say, Nelson's Column in one hour.' Hugh found himself breathless, even faint, at having to give Margaret these instructions.

She looked at him, tolerant and amused, and tipped ash onto the ground in a way that Hugh, even in this situation, could not help finding improper.

'Oh I say, Hugh, don't be feeble. Lilibet is perfectly all right. After all, she's not a child. She's just gone for a walk. She will have just gone for a … a stroll and then back to the Palace. Honestly, what did you think would happen if we got separated?'

Margaret herself started to walk in the direction of the Mall; Hugh had no choice but to follow her. Faces and bodies loomed at them from the dusk, and bonfires caused fragments of charred paper to flutter over their heads, as if from a distant volcano. Firefly-points of lit cigarettes dotted the gloom – one of these bobbed periodically from Margaret's mouth to her waist.

After ten minutes, they found themselves under Admiralty Arch. There was no chance of finding Elizabeth, Hugh could see that now. He had gone into a numbed state, but one in which the question of what profession he would follow in peacetime stood out with painful clarity. Soldiering was out.

'No,' said Margaret. 'No, I can't see her. Can *you* see her?'

Of course he couldn't. Nobody could. She was lost in the crowds. But it was very uncharacteristic of Elizabeth simply to walk off like that. Earlier, she had been the one who was anxiously shepherding their group. What did that mean? Hugh swallowed down the panic-python slithering up his throat.

'I really do think we can still separate, look for Her Royal Highness and then meet up at an agreed time and place.'

'Don't be absurd.'

Paralysed in this stalemate, they both gazed at the pavement, submitting tensely to the shouts and jostles of the rowdy passers-by. Some minutes passed like this.

'Well, look,' said Margaret, and she flicked away the cigarette. 'It's quite clear to me that Elizabeth has been looking for us in all this mess and she has given up. Gone back. Which is what we should do.'

There was something in that. Hugh had to admit it. In all probability, Elizabeth had already turned up at the Palace. He was already in trouble. It had already happened. The catastrophic end of his career in the army had already happened. And this being the case, all he could do now was make it worse by prolonging their absence. Perhaps, he wondered, Margaret herself would say to Their Majesties that Elizabeth had insisted on striking out on her own. It was possible that she would want to minimise her own culpability in this way.

'Yes, very good, Your Highness. Let's return to the Palace now.'

Some people in the crowd were beginning to look twice at Margaret and talk urgently among themselves, but still no one spoke to them. Hugh began to walk back, and Margaret looked at him contemptuously.

'*I* want to get a *cab*.'

Eight

Crash!

Mr Ware swept the empty glasses off the table with his left hand and lunged at Group Captain Brook with the broken Bass bottle that he clutched in his right.

'Christ. Steady on.'

Brook dodged to one side, colliding with Colin who was staggering away from the table, towards the bar. The edge of the table impeded Mr Ware's forward movement and the jagged edge of the bottle stopped well clear of where Brook's head would have been.

'Fucking nance. How dare you?'

'Argh.'

Attempting to shove the table out of the way, Mr Ware banged it hard against the legs of Brook as he was taking evasive action. The impact evidently infuriated him, and he picked up a chair, intending to throw it at Mr Ware, but it slipped out of his damp and slippery grip, and hit Colin reasonably hard on his side as he was timidly scurrying along the bar, trying to find some opening to go through, and duck down and hide, as the barman was now already doing.

'You filthy sod. How dare you?'

'To hell with you.'

Brook flung the ashtray at Mr Ware; its powdery grey contents made a vapour trail, which then disintegrated and descended. The ashtray itself ricocheted off Mr Ware's forehead, and this assault was clearly far more successful than the aggressor anticipated.

'Ow! Argh! Cunt!'

Menacingly, his murderous indignation evidently redoubled,

and holding one hand up to his injured head, Mr Ware advanced on Brook with his broken bottle in the other hand. Brook, though still defiant, backed away, unaware that he was being manoeuvred into a corner. His sneer was kept in place very materially due to something that Brook could see and that Mr Ware could not. Ginnie, the manageress, was advancing on him from behind in a stealthy manner very similar to that with which she had crept up on him just an hour before. But now her face was set like cement. She held a cricket bat. The men in the club looked on, awed by her imminent intervention.

With a mighty sweep, Ginnie brought the bat down, not on Mr Ware's head, but on the hand holding the bottle. It dropped. In the same instant, and with practised expertise, Ginnie dropped her bat, grabbed Mr Ware's right wrist with her left hand, twisted it sharply behind his back and with the other arm got him round his throat in a choke-hold.

Both dropped to their knees.

'Now, darling, are you going to calm down, or must I break your arm?'

Mr Ware shook his head, his eyes on the floor.

'Does that mean, no, you're not going to calm down, or, no, you'll not make any trouble?'

'No trouble. Not make trouble.'

'Well, all right then.'

Ginnie released him, standing and theatrically splaying out her palms as she stepped back. Mr Ware clutched his painful right shoulder. Group Captain Brook's face was very white. His hair was tousled and his arms and shoulders were shaking. But he was still confident enough to be indignant.

'Intolerable. Intolerable. Madman.'

'What was, darling?' Ginnie looked over to him. Everyone else in the bar was still looking at them. The broken bottle still lay on the floor at Ginnie's feet.

'One makes a joke. A simple joke. One never intended the smallest offence.'

'That what it was?'

Ginnie was looking over at Colin who was looking away, at an angle, at the floor, his doughy face scrunched with anxiety. He shrugged.

'Now, dearest,' Ginnie directed this at Mr Ware himself. 'I want you to pick up that bottle and put it in the bin behind the bar. Will you do that for me?'

Cowed, obedient, Mr Ware got up, gingerly picked up the bottle between finger and thumb and disposed of it as Ginnie had requested. He stood still, awaiting further orders. She went over to him and gently placed her hand on his tense, quivering shoulder.

'Darling. I'd like you to go away from here and take a bit of a constitutional. No one's throwing you out. We all can have a row now and then. It doesn't matter. No one gets upset, not really. Everyone here's got skin like elephant hide. You're always welcome here, you know that, and I know how much you've done for the place. But really on tonight of all nights, everything has to be sweetness and light. Do you know what I mean?'

Mr Ware nodded, his lips compressed tightly. Colin thought he might be about to cry.

'Now, why don't you get a breath of fresh air?'

Mr Ware duly made his way to the exit, and caught a glimpse of Group Captain Brook incautiously smiling with relief and triumph, a smile which was smartly wiped from his face, as Mr Ware glared directly at him.

None of the men on the door looked Mr Ware in the eye as he left, lighting another cigarette.

It really was dark outside now, though there was an electric light on, and the metal-grille door-hatch was now securely bolted back as he climbed back up the metal stairs and up to pavement level.

Mr Ware fancied that the darkness was intensified by the crush of people in the Soho streets. There was a whooping and cheering as the crowd saluted a foursome which paraded along Great Windmill Street: dressed up as Churchill, Stalin and then another white man and then a Chinaman. It was only once they had passed him that Mr Ware could identify this last two from the names they had written on their backs: General Smuts and General Chiang Kai-Shek. There were Poles, French. He heard a babble of non-English voices. Very pretty women were walking along on the arms of Americans.

One was saying, 'The extraordinary thing is that I was at the Berlin Games in '36. I had tea with the Duke of Saxe-Coburg-Gotha at his villa, on the day of the opening ceremony. My brother was at school with him. The very day. It was less than ten years ago. Think of that.'

Everyone was very far gone. Mr Ware, who could drink a fair bit without it affecting him physically, couldn't help feeling intoxicated in the way he always did at the sight of other people becoming vulnerable. He wondered if he might try taking someone's wallet. Maybe. Lot of uniforms about. Not as easy as civvy gear: suits, topcoats.

Mr Ware walked and, as he did so, indulged in his mannerism of grinning and winking at every third or fourth person his eyes met. The posher they were, the better bred, the more readily and politely they attempted to return his smile, thinking that they had met at some stage. It was his way of determining the social class of complete strangers, determining how much cash they were likely to have on them.

He was still angry – or rather, his anger was still there, but being converted into something else. Into energy and determination. And he was talking rapidly to himself, another habit that he had had since childhood, and which showed no sign of fading. That Brook fellow. How dare he make those remarks? As if they were friends. As if they were intimates, business associates. Something strange about him. Group Captain? Group Captain my aching tootsie. If Brook was a Group Captain in the RAF, then Mr Ware was a member of the Sadler's Wells ballet. His arm hurt where Ginnie had beat it down with the bat; his other arm hurt where she had twisted it up behind his back, and his throat hurt from where she'd all but throttled him. Mr Ware supposed that he should have known Ginnie would do something like that to him. He had seen her do it to other men in the club often enough. Never at the start of the evening, though.

In Brewer Street, two drunk Welshmen were playing leapfrog on the pavement, like schoolboys, one over the other, all the way down the street. A boisterous crowd swarmed by them, cheering. In the window of a bookshop, a tattered notice read, 'Second Front Now' with a picture of Stalin. In the alley that ran alongside it, Mr Ware could see a prostitute giving hand-relief to someone in uniform. This fellow out on the town spoiling himself, was he? Or perhaps he was down from the provinces for the day to get his British Empire Medal. Or perhaps it wasn't a prostitute – who could tell? – perhaps it was his sweetheart, perhaps it was someone he'd met for the first time on this magical night of all nights. This was a lovely little anecdote to tell their grandchildren. A pool of light revealed them only partially, but Mr Ware could see his kitbag and coat bundled on the ground; the woman had her back to Mr Ware, murmuring into the chap's ear and he of course had his eyes shut. Instinctively, Mr Ware wondered if he could pinch the man's gear, and began to creep up; her wrist was going like the clappers, the fellow's knees were sagging and there would never be a better time than now, but he wouldn't have more than half a minute at the outside. He stepped further into the alley and looked around – no one there. Stealthily, he approached, close enough to hear what she was saying.

'There. There. There.'

He came in closer. The woman had her free hand splayed up against the brickwork to her right; her customer's back was up against the wall. Mr Ware was close enough to see the man was chewing on the corner of a handkerchief.

Whump.

Mr Ware's jaw slackened as he felt a hand on his shoulder, still painful anyway. The police?

'Hello!'

It was Colin, smiling shyly. His greeting, absurdly loud, coincided with a strangled yelp from the man in the alley; the woman had retreated. Neither had noticed Mr Ware, who now stepped back out into the street.

'Colin. What the bloody hell do you want?'

Mr Ware was unsettled enough to give Colin a fourpenny one, right then and there.

'You forgot these.' Colin's voice was gentle, reproachful. He held up Mr Ware's bag, with his ARP overalls and helmet. He had forgotten them; left them behind in the club. Colin had followed him all the way out here, to give it back to him. He really ought to be grateful.

'Oh. Well, thank you very much Colin.'

'Not at all, old thing. Evening!'

Colin was politely greeting the woman emerging from the alley, who was making a brisk exit, having told her mark to wait behind for a moment, for all the world as if she was an office worker heading for the Underground at the end of a long day.

'Devil of a job finding you, old boy.'

'Mm.'

'But I just about knew your haunts. They're my haunts as well!'

'Yes.'

'Evening!'

Now the customer was coming out. Mr Ware could see his handkerchief coming out of his right hip pocket. Didn't know what a close shave he'd had. He looked refreshed, calm.

'Bad business back there in the Club, old thing.'

'Well yes, I suppose so.'

'You know what a temper you've got. If you're thinking of looking in again, you'd better stay amicable.'

'Yes.'

'Group Captain Brook was only trying to make a joke, to be pleasant.'

Mr Ware was silent.

'I say, let's go to the Blue Post for a drink.'

Of course, that place was packed, but some men had dragged the upright piano out into the street for a singsong; many patrons had excitedly followed and so it wasn't as crowded as it might have been.

Colin bought Mr Ware another pint of Bass and a packet of cigarettes, assuming that these would have a temporarily calming effect, and they did. He had also got them half of a pork pie. They made short work of that.

'You know ...'

'Yes?'

'You know, I don't think we should go out on a job tonight, old thing.'

'Why not?'

'Well, frankly I don't want to work. I just want to relax. I want to relax the way everyone else is relaxing.' Colin gestured around at all the drunk people, singing. 'I'm sitting here, drinking beer, but it's having no effect on me, because I can't stop thinking about it. And I rather think tonight might be my last opportunity in a while to, er, *socialise.*'

'Well don't then,' said Mr Ware shortly. 'Don't come. You're not much use in civvies anyway. I'd rather have someone in uniform. That would make it look better.'

'But, look, it's just getting dangerous. I worry about you.'

'Worry?' Mr Ware snorted. 'Don't worry.' As if weighing in on his side, the drinkers sang:

What's the point of worrying?
It never was worthwhile.

Glumly, Colin pressed a damp forefinger to his greasy plate and transferred fragments of pork pie to his tongue. Mr Ware lit them both cigarettes and passed one to him. They smoked, and Colin started worrying again about the wine business and how on earth he was going to make a go of that. Would the end of rationing make a difference? Mr Ware was talking to two young women, betting them that he could arrange five matches so as to make two triangles. Having won that bet, and sportingly declined to take any money, he bet them he could rearrange the order of three coins while touching them only five times. The wager he now playfully suggested was a kiss. The two women giggled while Colin looked dispirited. Mr Ware stabbed adroitly at the coins with his thumb a number of times; he appeared to win his bet on a technicality, but again did not insist on his winnings.

Instead, he leant over to the first girl and told her, 'You know, I have this remarkable gift. I can tell what someone's star sign is, just by gazing deeply into their eyes.'

'Go on!'

'I can. It's the truth.'

They both giggled, and the first allowed Mr Ware to lean forwards and look directly at her. 'You mustn't blink, or this isn't going to work.'

With calm candour, Mr Ware placed his face close to hers, and despite his instruction she blinked and flinched and tittered while he kept his gaze commandingly steady.

'I think ... you're an Aries.'

'Oh my Gawd! You're right!'

'Is he, Jane?'

'He is. Eileen, he is. He's dead on.'

Without them noticing, Mr Ware silently placed Jane's identity card, with her date of birth, back into her bag.

'I can see the Zodiacal constellations in your irises, Jane, you see. But there's something else. I can tell straight away that you're a passionate, loving person but that you haven't been treated as you deserve by a certain man. Is that right? Oh, dear. I can't read your star sign if we're going to get the waterworks, you know.'

Jane looked down and a single tear fell like a raindrop, splat, onto a beermat. Soon she was quietly sniffling, while he stroked her hand.

'You attract men who are not worthy of you,' Mr Ware continued while she nodded miserably. 'And you have family worries which you are too proud to share with your friends.'

'That means my mum,' she said to Eileen.

She was clearly awed by this insight, and Mr Ware changed the subject, sensing that it was becoming too tragic. He now said, 'But there's an older man who's a bit besotted with you.'

Her friend yelped with laughter. 'Mr Ainsworth!'

They both shrieked. Mr Ware took out a cigarette packet and offered it to Jane and Eileen and they both accepted. This too appeared to be an indulgence they were permitting themselves on this special night. Eileen was evidently an accomplished smoker; Jane was however soon coughing alarmingly and Mr Ware thumped her on the back as she bent over.

'Ha! Now you're getting it. We'll have you smoking like a chimney in no time. With a bit of practice, you'll be doing this. Look.' Mr Ware took her cigarette and blew three perfect smoke rings. 'Ooo!' he spelled them out, insidiously.

'What lovely hands *you* have,' he then said, turning to Eileen. 'I can tell a lot about you from your hands.'

'Like what, indeed?'

'Lovely smooth hands. But do you see the way your lifeline is broken here and here?'

'Yes?'

'It means family difficulties. That means you're worried about someone close to you.'

'Well,' she said tartly, 'I can tell a lot about *you* from *your* hands.'

'Ho yes? Like what?'

'You're divorced. Or you're separated. Terribly unhappy, anyway.'

Mr Ware looked at her sharply, suspiciously.

'What do you mean?'

'You've taken your wedding ring off. Recently. Look.'

Mr Ware's puffy ringer bore a red-looking ridge where the ring had been.

Icily, suddenly, Mr Ware got up, scraping his chair back. It was enough to make a few people look over, despite the din and the gloom and the music. He plunged his hand into his pocket and jingled the change.

'Checking that you've still got it?' asked Eileen, shrewdly. This was evidently more than Mr Ware could take.

'Well, it's been very nice talking to you,' he choked, his playful teasing now utterly abandoned.

'Off home to your wife, perhaps?' said Eileen, cruelly pursuing her advantage. 'Do give her our best.'

Without another word, Mr Ware turned on his heel and walked out. Colin gulped down the rest of his drink and followed.

*

In Broadwick Street, a mixed group of servicemen and civilians were attempting a human pyramid. Three strong-looking men along the base and two more on their quivering shoulders. Then, to form the apex, a woman in WAAF uniform was hitching up her skirts and trying to leap onto the middle pair, who were each holding one of her hands. She herself had been standing on a car roof, which had begun to dent. With a final leap, she was up, to a huge cheer. But then, wobble, wobble, wobble, and the whole formation collapsed and the WAAF fell, and looked as if she had hurt herself really quite badly. Somehow even this couldn't cheer Mr Ware up.

Nine

Margaret sat up in bed, drinking cocoa. Bliss. She was reading the latest *Picturegoer*. Everything was calm now. It turned out that Elizabeth had not in fact returned to the Palace quite yet. When they discovered this, some of the staff had got in a fearful bate with Hugh. Some of them were even saying that he should report to Their Majesties himself. Poor Hugh had gone quite pale and said nothing. But then she, Margaret, had had a brainwave. She told everyone not to worry, it was just that she herself wanted to come home early but Elizabeth wanted to stop out half an hour longer, and that Peter was naturally with her, and it was all perfectly in order.

What a cheeky fib. Margaret had actually caught Hugh's eye while she was saying it, letting him know that she had jolly well saved his bacon! Hugh even nodded once, and sort of turned that into a tiny submissive bow, and then said loudly that he would go back out and 'rejoin Peter' and that he was sure they would all be back soon.

Well, of course they would! What a lot of silly fuss.

Margaret considered. If there really *was* a row about tonight, she would just come up with a couple more fibs. Muddy the waters. She could say that Henry Porchester was with them. Porchy. Porchy would back them up. Porchy was a good egg.

Here was an advertisement for Pond's cold cream. 'It's still no easy matter to get hold of well-known and trusted creams, such as Pond's – only a proportion of the pre-war supply is allowed to be made,' it said. 'It should be used as sparingly as possible.'

Margaret looked complacently at the colossal pot of Pond's on her dressing table. She snuggled further down under the covers, scissoring her legs deliciously against the linen, and continued to read.

Mickey Rooney, it seemed, was getting paid a bonus of £40,000 by MGM – 'It is typical of the generosity MGM executives have always shown towards Mickey, who is regarded as "their own boy", since he was practically raised on the MGM lot.'

Goodness, forty thousand pounds, what a lot of money.

'Was Lilibet having a good time?' Margaret wondered.

She imagined that she *was* having a good time. Or even if she wasn't, she would begin to enjoy herself by and by. Heavens, how stuffy Lilibet could be sometimes, and how often she forced one into situations where one had to be stuffy as well. Well, now the boot was on the other foot. Now she had put Lilibet into a jolly situation and now Lilibet had to be jolly for once in her life. It was a requirement, like gas masks. Gosh, gas masks. They hadn't needed them after all, had they? Where *was* her gas mask, come to think of it?

Outside, in the far distance, she could hear more singing: 'I Belong to Glasgow'.

Margaret read that the Army Pictorial Service had invited soldiers stationed in the Middle East to write in with suggestions telling the film industry what's what. The winning letter – the chap had got £15 – was from Private JB Steckley of the US Air Corps, who wrote: '1. War. (a) Lay off it (b) If you must show us war, show us our Allies. When we see what they are going through, we'll be twice as glad that it isn't happening at home.'

No. Well, it isn't happening at home. Not any more. The war is over.

It's all over.

Margaret finished her cocoa and replaced the empty mug by her bed. She scraped with her thumbnail at a tiny, dried tide-mark at the lip.

What was Lilibet doing now? Well, soon she would be back to tell Margaret herself. Margaret expected a sharp knock on her door at any moment, a very cross demand for an explanation. Well, it wasn't her fault.

Margaret turned off the light and lay staring at the ceiling on which some light pooled from the window. What would she do tomorrow? Margaret couldn't imagine. She shut her eyes, and still couldn't. She would return to the schoolroom, but Lilibet wouldn't have to. Margaret saw Lilibet floating through their schoolroom like a balloon, and realised that she was drifting off and beginning to dream. She awoke, exhaling heavily through her nose, turned off the bedside light and fell asleep before she could remove the *Picturegoer* from her pillow.

Ten

Katharine and Elizabeth were in the ladies' cloakroom at the Ritz. The object of the exercise, as Katharine briskly put it, was to get her friend cleaned up, and ready to confront the world. While Elizabeth washed her face, Katharine had her jacket in her hand, attacking it smartly with a stiff clothes brush which the attendant had lent her, and who continued to sit by the door with a saucer of silver coins pointedly displayed: she had seen him in the act of weeding out some coppers and putting them in his pocket. Elizabeth had her glasses on the cabinet surface by the basin while she splashed her face with water, head bowed slightly, not looking at herself in the mirror.

'Don't you ever take those off?' asked Katharine.

'Blind as a bat without them.' Elizabeth tried to shrug while bent over; the effect was of a brief, convulsive hunch. She towelled herself, restored the glasses in such a way that her hands covered much of her face, pulled on the proffered jacket.

'You must let me put some makeup on you, you know,' said Katharine; she firmly removed the glasses again, and applied eyeliner while Elizabeth submitted.

'You know,' said Katharine, 'now you'll think me awfully tight, but you remind me dreadfully of someone.'

'I know exactly what you're going to say,' said Elizabeth smoothly, as she put the glasses back on, and ducking past, left the ladies' room, leading the way. 'Everybody says it. You'll doubtless see a lot of people looking at me twice. It's Margaret Lockwood. I look very much like Margaret Lockwood.'

'Really?'

'Oh yes. Margaret Lockwood. It's a queer thing, I know, but there it is.'

Soon they were back in the chaotic crush of merry-makers and inebriates in the hotel, and Elizabeth glanced at Katharine, just as she was glancing sidelong at her. But she seemed satisfied with this explanation.

'You stay here, and I'll get us a drink.'

Elizabeth positioned herself uneasily next to a large potted plant, and by appearing to check her wristwatch, turning away periodically from the throng and putting it up to her ear, she went unnoticed. It was only once Katharine had gone that she realised that she had no idea what drink she was going to get. Predictably, Katharine reappeared with gins.

'You know, Lil,' she said, 'I think you're much prettier than Margaret ...'

'Oh no,' interrupted Elizabeth modestly, and added without thinking, 'she's much prettier and she always has Papa in fits of laughter.'

'What?'

'Oh. Oh, sorry, I was thinking how much my father likes Margaret Lockwood films.'

'Oh, I see.'

'Anyway, I've got the doings, here's how.'

'Thanks, jolly good!'

Two Americans came over and offered to buy them drinks, and were smoothly rebuffed by Katharine. Elizabeth sipped at her gin, and confided, 'I'm actually supposed to be out with my sister, at the moment, but I'm afraid I got separated from her, and the two chaps we were with.'

'Oh. Her boyfriend and your fiancé?'

'No, just some nice Guards officers who'd offered to accompany us for the evening.'

'Well! Lil, you dark horse!'

'Oh no, it was nothing like that, really it wasn't.'

'Huh! A likely tale!' Katharine slightly slapped Elizabeth's elbow with the back of her hand to show that she was joshing. 'Well, out of the frying pan ...' she added mysteriously. 'What's your fiancé's name, actually?'

'It's … it's Pip.'

'Pip?'

'Yes, Pip.'

'As in Dickens?'

'Mm. And what's your husband called?'

'He's called William.'

'And what does he do for a living?'

'Oh, he's frightfully high up in the Home Office. I just never see him, but now there's not a war on I expect everything will be returned to normal.'

'I expect so.'

'Well … Pip. You and Pip. Lil and Pip. On the road to matrimony. Like a Bob Hope picture, isn't it? Where's Pip now anyway?'

'He's onboard ship.'

'Girl in every port?'

'Oh no!' Elizabeth shook her head and drank some more.

'I say, Lil,' Katharine suddenly became serious. 'You know what we were saying before? About the wedding night?'

Elizabeth nodded.

'Well, will the groom be approaching this in a similar … a similar state of …'

Elizabeth realised that this, along with their honeymoon destination, was something about which she had no idea. Katharine placed a delicate hand on her wrist.

'Oh, my dear. I've no wish to embarrass you. The point is that the situation is completely different for a man. It is the man's duty to gain experience. Probably with a professional. Do you know what I mean?'

Elizabeth didn't.

'Very often,' Katharine continued, speaking in a trance of worldliness, 'a man's father or uncle will arrange for him to meet a professional, often in France.'

Baffled, Elizabeth assumed that she meant a medical professional, some sort of genito-urinary specialist.

'My own husband has seen the world, a lot of the world,'

continued Katharine, and again Elizabeth now noticed how her new friend's manner would veer between knowing, girlish intimacy and a glassy-eyed reverence for what she imagined to be the norms and conventions of society. 'When we met, he was ... well, he was attached. Engaged, actually.'

'Ah,' said Elizabeth, not sure how to reply.

'He was *engaged*, yes,' Katharine reasserted, as if clearing up, for good and all, an evasive ambiguity which others had been trying to foist on her. 'We met in Pangbourne. It was just before the war. His people had a place there.'

'Yes?'

'There was a party at his parents' house. William was there and *she* was there too. Now, I know what you're thinking.'

'Well,' said Elizabeth politely, 'it is rather late, and I suppose I was just wondering if I ought to be getting ba—'

'You're thinking that this was *actually the engagement party itself*. That I had insinuated myself into someone else's home and nabbed another girl's man. Not a bit of it. I actually found William rather a bore at first.'

Katharine now looked around, and said, 'Do you suppose we shall ever find somewhere to sit down?'

'Well, I—'

'Anyway, I arrived on my own. And do you know what struck me first about William? His eyes. Those terribly sad spaniel eyes!' Katharine laughed convulsively, like a sneeze, and for the first time Elizabeth realised how far gone she was. 'How I used to tease him afterwards about his poor-me look!'

She was continuing to scan the room, but there were no free tables.

'I knew he was unhappy. And the woman he was with, well! She was clingy and destructive. And frankly she wasn't quite the thing, do you know what I mean? Perhaps William had thought it frightfully romantic to get engaged to someone like that. But actually it wasn't practical at all. How on earth she supposed to mix socially with William's people? Oh, no. It wouldn't do at all. What about *that* one?'

Katharine pointed sharply at a table which appeared to be empty, but no. A rowdy group of Canadians got there first.

'Anyhow, I could tell that William was discontented. He began to confide in me almost from that very first evening. I sat next to her father at dinner: an awful old bore, and a nasty piece of work at that. He actually put his hand on my thigh during the meal; I stuck his leg with a fork. He let out a yelp and had to pretend he'd been stung by a *wasp*!'

Katharine laughed fondly at the memory.

'"What wasp?" said his wife, a terrible old dragon. "Wasp I tell you!" he shouted and went out to bathe his leg under cold water, though the silly old fool had to pretend it was wrist because nobody would believe a wasp could sting him through his trousers, not that anyone believed him in any case. Anyway, our eyes met. William could sense that something was going on; he could sense that I had asserted myself and he respected me for it. I was also wearing an extremely low-cut gown.'

'Was William working for the Home Office at that time?' enquired Elizabeth politely.

'Oh, yes. He was. Anyway, it was a fine summer's night and everyone mingled in the back garden after dinner; there were candles on stalks and they had staff bringing round glasses of pudding wine on trays. It was rather ghastly actually, but anyway that's when William introduced himself. His fiancée was – well, she was somewhere else. Perhaps she was up in the bathroom, attending to her poor papa's wasp-sting. Do you want a cigarette, incidentally?'

Katharine held out a packet to her. Elizabeth considered. Margo had claimed recently to have smoked a cigarette, but Elizabeth didn't believe her, and of course they had had a quarrel about it. It was precisely the sort of thing they were always arguing about these days, and these days Margaret appeared, irritatingly, to be somehow overtaking Elizabeth in the growing-up stakes, to be more knowing about the ways of the world.

'All right, yes, thank you.' She took one and demurely put the wrong end in her mouth, with the filter-tip pointing out. What an odd taste. Katharine wordlessly removed it, turned it round, re-inserted it. Then she asked a passing waiter if he had a light. Smoothly, the man produced a lighter from his hip pocket; the tiny flame kissed the tip of both their cigarettes and Elizabeth wondered how she knew how to suck in at the moment of lighting. She was not so foolish as to try to suck down the smoke into her lungs directly; instead she swirled it around her mouth and gently exhaled. The mild euphoria had nothing to do with nicotine: Elizabeth had passed herself off as a member of the glamorous smoking classes. She placed the cigarette between her middle and index finger and held her hand steady over the glass, marvelling at how easily these gestures came to her: discreetly twirling hand movements as formal and yet relaxed as those of a flamenco dancer. She took another gulp of gin and found herself smiling, almost grinning, at what Katharine was saying.

'William was showing me around the garden – although what right he had to do that, I don't know. It was clear he just wanted to get me on my own. We walked off from the group, talking of this and that. I rather boldly asked him if he was unhappy, and he said he was. So handsome. My dear, you mustn't be shocked. We kissed right then and there. He took me round the waist like *this* –'

She took Elizabeth round the waist with her right arm, her left hand adroitly holding drink and cigarette.

'And kissed me like *this* –'

Katharine kissed Elizabeth for the second time, and Elizabeth now realised that their position behind the large plant obscured their clinch from the view of the other drinkers. She struggled and squeaked, trying also to smile indulgently, but was on the point of relaxing, when Katharine suddenly released her and continued:

'My dear, I wriggled and wriggled, just like that, but William was so passionate. It was clear to me his engagement was at end. We were married at Christmas. Now. Isn't that a romantic story?'

'Excuse me, miss.'

Katharine turned around and appeared highly irritated and displeased to find a man with sandy, receding hair, heavy bags under his eyes, and a slight squint. Elizabeth could see that one of his eyes looked straight ahead, and the other turned out. Like everyone else here, he was clearly incapable.

'I saw that you two ladies had nowhere to sit, and I wondered if you would like to join me and my friend? And I can't let a girl in uniform stand around in discomfort. The name's Ware.' The man smiled and held out his hand. Elizabeth shook it.

'Well, Mr Ware,' she said, decisively forestalling what she assumed would be Katharine's rebuff, 'thank you. That would be very kind. Come on Katharine!'

Mr Ware turned on his heel and Elizabeth followed; after a beat, so did Katharine. Through the murky crush, they found that this man did indeed have a table, a cramped square table that the staff had evidently used for drinks or stacking plates, but which had now, on this special night, been commandeered for the customers. There was someone else there, too, an older, balding man in a chalkstripe suit, slumped rather miserably. Elizabeth noticed that, as the evening wore on, about one in a dozen of the people she had seen that night were actually in the grip of intense, frozen misery, like gaunt statues around which heedless people danced.

'Ah!' said Mr Ware, briskly. 'This is my friend Colin. He was just being a bit of a bore on the subject of how he will fare as a wine merchant in peacetime. For Gawd's sake, buck up Colin.'

'Awfully sorry,' said Colin, grinning sheepishly and apologetically. 'He's quite right. Now's not the time to talk about that. I'm Colin Erskine-Jones. How do you do? Very pleased to make your acquaintance.'

Katharine and Elizabeth introduced themselves and sat down, and Katharine appeared to have resumed her air of someone cheerfully out on the town, game for anything.

'Apart from anything else, Colin had better get into a better mood,' said Mr Ware, briefly checking his watch. 'He's putting on an entertainment later on for one and all.'

Elizabeth asked, politely, 'Really? Are you, Mr Erskine-Jones?'

'Oh yes, that,' grimaced Colin. 'It's really nothing.'

'Ho no it isn't,' said Mr Ware, 'it's quite something. You two ladies play your cards in the correct manner and you could witness one of the most remarkable amateur talents in London.'

'Now I really am intrigued,' said Katharine smoothly.

The conversation lulled for a moment, and Colin suddenly narrowed his eyes and leaned forwards. 'You know, you have a look of someone ...'

'Yes,' said Elizabeth smartly, 'Margaret Lockwood. Everyone says so. Listen to that.' For the first time, they listened to a trio of piano, bass and accordion thumping out dance tunes in the din. The noise and crush had almost drowned them. 'I say, Mr Ware,' said Elizabeth impulsively, 'would you like to dance?'

For the tiniest fraction of a second, Mr Ware looked affronted at this presumption, suspecting a tease. Then he replaced this expression with one of roguish wonder.

'Goodness me,' he piped schoolmarmishly. 'What an inversion of the natural order of things! Are you asking, miss?'

'I am.'

'Well, all right then.'

Elizabeth could not, if pressed, define exactly the mood that led her to do this; she was rather merry and careless, and this was a diversionary tactic, yes, but this man was actually now more likely to see through her disguise. She had almost decided she wanted to see what would happen when people knew that it was really her. She had seen people looking at her twice. Perhaps they had guessed. People in London did not pester people they recognised, Elizabeth thought. Bobo said that even Mr Churchill could walk across St James's Park, on his own, without being stopped.

Mr Ware clamped Elizabeth firmly to him and they proceeded to whirl around the floor, in a frantic two-step.

'I do love a girl in uniform!' said Mr Ware.

'Thank you.'

'What uniform is that?'

'I'm in the ATS.'

'Huh?' asked Mr Ware, puzzled.

'Why aren't you in khaki, actually?'

'Well ...' said Mr Ware, 'On the trot, see?'

'I'm so sorry, I don't underst—'

'Watch it, pal. Have a heart,' Mr Ware was remonstrating with a man who had just cannoned into him, and then blundered away without replying. For a long moment, Mr Ware just stared after him, his face a plump, dead mask of hostility.

'I don't understand,' persisted Elizabeth. 'On the trot?'

Mr Ware recovered his good humour.

'Oh. Oh well.' He had decided to be coy. 'I retired from the services. I invalided myself out. Army life didn't suit me. It was my nerves.'

'Nerves?'

'I was extremely nervous about getting shot by a German.'

Mr Ware laughed immoderately, and Elizabeth found herself laughing too, without knowing why. The room continued to whirl after the music finished and they stopped moving.

'Shall we return to our table, my dear?' asked Mr Ware, with an elaborate bow, 'I have a treat in mind.'

On regaining their former places, they found Colin and Katharine attempting to tear up their ration books.

'We won't be needing these any more!' sang out Katharine gaily.

'Not half!'

Mr Ware removed a matchbox from his pocket, and, like a schoolboy with a contraband frog, slid open the drawer to show Elizabeth its contents. They looked like six or seven squashed black pellets of something or other. Elizabeth was baffled.

'Here you are,' said Mr Ware, with a wink. 'These'll pep you up.'

'I say,' said Colin. 'Steady on.'

'Steady on? Steady *on*? You steady on, if you like. You've got a show to do. We're here to celebrate.'

He produced a cigarette, and with a pencil shoved one of the pellets into the end; it made some of the tobacco fall out, and gave it an odd, misshapen, bulbous look. Then he lit it, inhaling deeply with a roguish smile. The smell was sweet and sharp and made some of the other people look over at their table, curiously, and then look away.

'Well, you can jolly well give me a drag,' said Katharine urgently. 'Come on.' She gave Mr Ware a sharp dig in the ribs with her fingertips and he passed the cigarette to her. Elizabeth wondered how she could be so familiar with a casual acquaintance, one whom, just ten minutes ago, she didn't seem all that keen to get to know. Katharine took two quick puffs – the end glowed intensely with a throb – and her face assumed the same dopey, beatific look as Mr Ware's. She offered the cigarette to Colin, who waved it away. Then she offered it to Elizabeth.

'What is it?' asked Elizabeth.

'A pick-me-up,' said Mr Ware, smiling at her. 'A little stimulant. I take them for my nerves, but they're good for anyone. Colin's mother takes them for her irritable bowels. Athletes take them before a big race. I know for a fact that Mr Churchill took one at the Casablanca conference. Try it.'

Elizabeth took the cigarette, sucked and spat out the smoke.

'You've got to take the smoke *in*,' giggled Katharine, and Elizabeth thought: How does she know all about it? But she puffed again, and tried to keep the smoke down. This she was able to do without any mortifying splutters and coughs. There was a brief pause, and her head swam. She felt Katharine's hand on her knee; it then moved companionably up her inner thigh, and caressed it. Elizabeth fancied she could hear the nylon shimmering and crackling. The three faces, now like moons or discs, grinned at her.

'Another gin?'

She had not the smallest idea who had asked her that, but another gin appeared in front of her, and Elizabeth drank, and the moon-faces chattered and giggled, in what seemed like a foreign language, Lithuanian or Portuguese. Katharine's hand was still on her thigh. Then Katharine kissed her again, and Elizabeth let her. She was wondering what Margo, Hugh and Peter were doing now. She was thinking about Philip. What was he doing now? When would he come ashore? And when was the first time he had kissed her? It had been at Windsor, before the war. They were both in civvies, anyway. He had actually initiated the process by putting a curled forefinger under her chin and raising her face to his. How Elizabeth's heart had hammered when she realised what was going to happen! The kiss had been gentle, mannerly, temperate, quite unlike the queer kiss that Katharine was giving her now. Afterwards, Philip had withdrawn his face, smiled and said, 'There.' Just that. Katharine finally herself withdrew, but said nothing and only took another drag at her strange cigarette. Her hand stayed on Elizabeth's thigh, now very high up.

'What numbers are you going to favour us with this evening, dear heart?' Mr Ware was saying brightly to Colin.

'I thought I might have a bash at "Darling Je Vous Aime".'

'Very good. I always like that one.'

'So do I,' said Katharine.

Suddenly, their table was jolted, disagreeably. They all looked up to see the same man who had bumped into Elizabeth and Mr Ware when they had been on the dance floor. He was clearly drunker than ever, and grinned unrepentantly.

'Sorry about that, old thing,' the man trilled, and with a free hand tousled Mr Ware's hair. Instantly, Elizabeth could feel Colin and Katharine shrink away from their companion – Katharine's hand disappeared from her thigh.

Mr Ware ground his cigarette into an ashtray, pursed his lips and stood up. He placed his right hand on the man's left arm as he was turning to go and, with what looked like simple physical force, compelled him to wheel back and face him.

'Ah, listen, *old thing.*'

'What is it, what do you want?'

'What do I want? My dear old thing, I want to dance with you!'

To the man's astonishment, Mr Ware switched the grip on his wrist – Elizabeth could see how he was pinching his skin – to his left hand and put his right around the man's waist. His new partner smiled uncertainly, unsure whether to play along with this prank and crucially failing to appreciate how both his hands had now been practically immobilised. Mr Ware grinned and raised his left foot, as if to lead his victim in a polka. But at the same time he tilted his head back, lifting his chin.

Katharine turned to Elizabeth and, with the forefinger and middle finger of one hand, actually turned her face away, so that she could not see what Mr Ware was doing. Elizabeth heard a sharp *smack* or *crack*, and turned back to see that Mr Ware was now standing back from the man, who now had both hands clamped over his face, and was squatting down on his haunches. Blood ran from his nose, as if from an open tap. People who were close enough to see had stopped dancing, and were looking on, and stepping back.

'*That's* what,' said Mr Ware coldly, and the crowds' retreat from him accelerated; Elizabeth could feel the colour of her face changing – Mr Ware's own face looked like piccalilli in this light – but she was still lucid enough to realise how the cigarette had anaesthetised her to what was happening. The music continued, the hubbub continued; it was almost possible to ignore all this, and as to what had actually happened between Mr Ware and the troublesome man, she was still blearily unsure. Both Colin and Katharine could see how two very large men in evening dress were now coming towards them. Mr Ware's victim was still hunched down, the blood pool around his feet widening in diameter every second. He was very still and quiet, and Elizabeth's ATS training was now telling her that he might be in shock, that he needed medical treatment immediately. In their very first week of instruction, ATS trainees had been told how apparently innocuous bumps on the head can lead to unconsciousness or even death. It was only in thinking about all this now that Elizabeth realised that Mr Ware had assaulted someone, and she should really call the police.

Eleven

The next thing Elizabeth knew, they were all in a taxi, with Mr Ware facing the rear windscreen, Colin opposite him and Katharine in the middle, next to Elizabeth, still stroking her thigh and nuzzling her neck, though more dopily and dozily now. Elizabeth herself was now kept awake by alternate waves of nausea and anxiety: when would she get home? Well, let's just see this Club they were talking about. Then she imagined she would just get another taxi. She would probably be home by, say, eleven or midnight at the latest. Elizabeth wondered uneasily if anyone back home was upset with her, and pushed these thoughts away into her mental fog.

'You and me, Lil!' Mr Ware was saying. He was pointing at his own chest and then at Elizabeth's. 'You and me. Tonight's the main event. And you and me are a vital part. An integral part. Ho yes. You wait.'

Elizabeth looked out of the window as the cab swept up to Piccadilly Circus and round into Shaftesbury Avenue. The VE celebrations now appeared to have taken on a rather different character. Everywhere she looked she saw men, young men, some in uniform, some in civvies, standing with their hands on their knees, looking down onto a pool of nameless mess. Some were holding their faces and noses, in exactly the posture Mr Ware's victim had been back at the Ritz. She could see couples who appeared to be dancing or spooning – as Elizabeth phrased it to herself – at every corner.

'Oh God,' said Colin.

An American army jeep had just braked sharply, on account of two men and a dog lurching out into the road. They could see the driver's head hit the windscreen with an audible smack and a continuous, simultaneous wail from the horn. Delayed themselves further ahead, the four could clearly see a diagonal crack in the jeep's windscreen, a line with what could have been a bulb of blood at either end. On the other side of the street, a group of men had smashed a shopwindow and were loading coats into a perambulator. Far away, a man was shouting, 'Victory in Japan! Victory in *Japan! Victory in Japan!'*

'I've got plans for you, Lil,' said Mr Ware, 'big plans. I need a girl in uniform for what I've got in mind.'

Katharine nuzzled. Elizabeth drowsed.

They arrived at the Butterfly Club in Great Windmill Street to find it transformed from the gloomy cavern in which Colin and Mr Ware had been drinking earlier in the evening. It was now packed and noisy. Mr Ware now had to present himself to be recognised by two big men by the trapdoor leading down, and having done so, he went smartly on ahead, without waiting to help the ladies down the steps. This was left to Colin.

The noise and music were far worse than in the Ritz. Mr Ware greeted the proprietress, whom he introduced as Ginnie, and they admired a large banner she had put up over the bar, reading 'Now for Japan'. Elizabeth listened to the snatches of conversation from the male patrons, which were as unintelligible as if they had been conducted in Swahili.

'I liked your companion the other night, dear. *She* was a bit of rough, wasn't she?'

'I take it with the smooth, dearest.'

'Was the rest of the evening *à deux*?'

'Can't you see the bruises?'

'Fishing for compliments, are we, *chérie*?'

'I was eating my meals off the mantelpiece for a week or so after *that* one, darling!'

'Your trousers are a positive cockpit of humanity, my dear; they are a Belgium of the spirit.'

'Stop it! Stop it!'

After some minutes of this, Mr Ware turned and introduced Elizabeth to his excitable and loquacious friend.

'Lil, let me present Tom Driberg. Tom, this is my friend, Lil.'

The man, tall, bulky, with receding, crinkly hair and sharp eyes, turned to her, and it was at this point that Elizabeth realised that she had been definitively recognised. Everyone else had been too drunk to be certain, or too shy to say, or it had been too crowded and chaotic and dark, or perhaps they had dimly sensed that on this night of all nights, appearances in the street from people like her were only to be expected.

Elizabeth held her hand out, frankly, to be shaken. Driberg's manner shifted into one of extreme deference and ostentatious tact. Smiling gently, as if taking possession of a secret, he took her hand very gently between his fingertips and bowed. Instinctively, Elizabeth turned her palm downward.

'Lil,' he said submissively, in a low voice. Mr Ware looked puzzled and turned away to talk to someone else.

'Mr Driberg,' returned Elizabeth, and then, 'Tom.' The covert reassumption of official duties awoke her, fractionally, from her bleary state. She looked around. Drinkers were standing shoulder to shoulder, and the room appeared to be in a rough L-shape. There was a bar along one side, and around the corner there was some sort of dance floor; directional lighting indicated the presence of a stage.

'How are you this evening, Tom?' she asked politely.

'Very well, indeed, Lil,' said Driberg, inclining his head somewhat. He, too, was obviously feeling the need to pull himself together after having had a good deal to drink. 'I wish you had been here earlier this evening. I could have introduced you to David Ben-Gurion. Such a nice man. I never knew anyone else who could impersonate a peewit using just his *tongue* and *teeth*, my dear. Ah, here is Noël.'

A well-built man with a slightly crooked nose and faintly pursed lips – with the air of someone perpetually tasting something unfamiliar – appeared at Driberg's side. He held his hand out with finger and thumb together, as if holding a champagne glass by the stem.

'Lil,' said Driberg, with that tone of proprietorial triumph which people always display on introducing an important new acquaintance to a status-conscious friend. 'Noël Coward. Noël, this is ...'

Instantly, Coward took Elizabeth's downturned palm in exactly the same way that Driberg had, tactfully, submissively, paying tribute to her pluck in being here, and not wishing to spoil the subterfuge.

'Lil,' he said with a quiet smile. 'I do hope that Driberg has not been boring you.'

'Not a bit,' said Elizabeth politely, and Driberg, disconcerted by his new friend taking this raillery seriously, added:

'Not the smallest bit. We were just talking about Proust.'

'Were you?'

'Were we?'

'Oh, yes. You surely will remember, my dear Noël, Marcel's descriptions of the blackout in Paris in the Great War, how it was the last time in history that the city's beauties could be appreciated by moonlight. I often thought of that passage during our recent blackouts, you know, walking home.'

'Was Proust uppermost in your mind on those occasions, my dear?'

'French literature *in the round*, dearest heart.'

'I'm so sorry, what?' said Elizabeth. 'It's so very noisy in here!'

Driberg was buffeted aside by someone carrying drinks to someone else, and a third person lunging across and kissing his girl, by taking her face in both hands. When the disturbance had passed, Coward appeared to have melted back into the crowd and Driberg was talking to a pale and petulant looking youth. He seemed to have forgotten she was there.

'Dearest,' he was saying. 'It will only take a moment. We would return to the fray instanter.'

'Shan't.'

'Perhaps a solatium of two pounds would make all the difference.'

'A what?'

'A gift of two pounds.'

'I don't want to miss the singer.'

'We won't.'

'I don't know that I want to ...'

'Dearest, it's very nutritional to me. It restores my vitamins. My iron levels. I have here a doctor's note' – he produced a tattered letter on which the crest of the Royal College of Physicians was visible – 'that says I have to have it.'

'Let me read that.'

'My dear, what would be the point? It's all in Latin.'

'Where's that three pounds?'

'Two pounds. I have it in my other coat, which is in the cloakroom. Come along.'

They left, and Coward reappeared at Elizabeth's side.

'Tell me, ah, *Lil*, if I may,' he said, 'how long have you known Driberg? Come to think of it,' and here his face clouded, 'how do you come to know all these –'

Ginnie, the proprietress, stood on a stool behind the bar, and shouted, 'The entertainments are about to commence!'

Everyone surged onto the dance floor; Elizabeth followed. She was sober enough, now, and determined to watch one or two songs and then get a cab home. Or perhaps Mr Coward would arrange a car for her.

Ginnie took the stage and approached the microphone.

'Ladies and gentlemen,' she declaimed. 'All the way from Paris.'

There was an outbreak of booing, and Elizabeth could hear some angry muttering of the word 'Pétain'.

'Come along, come on,' said Ginnie, tolerantly, and resumed: 'All the way from Paris. Please will you welcome our special VE Night *chanteuse*, Madame Kay L'Horreur!'

Some triumphant chords on the piano were thumped out, and then the audience was rewarded with the view of a plump woman who sashayed out onto the stage with a bizarrely emphatic hip-wiggling movement; so emphatic that Elizabeth thought she must have some sort of spinal injury. She wore a celebratory but blank smile, the sort that might be worn by a wax dummy; with a slow swivel of the head, her smile was directed first at Ginnie, and then at the cheering audience. Her makeup reflected the lighting in such a way as to make her face look two-dimensional, like a photograph. Her accompanist sat at the upright piano, with a self-effacing smile. Elizabeth managed to position herself at the back of the throng and at first thought that the woman looked so much like Colin that it was his sister or his mother. A rippling *arpeggio* from the piano merged into a *glissando* run up the keyboard and the woman twirled. Her unconvincing bodice, in profile, revealed to Elizabeth that it was a man; was in fact Colin himself. A ripple of applause and cheering swelled and then died as he approached the microphone and began to sing. Colin's singing voice had a pleasing quality, a light, quavering tenor, utterly unlike the hesitant mumble of his conversation.

Presently, to a loud cheer from everyone, the boy that Driberg had been talking to before the song began jumped up onto the stage and embraced Colin passionately. Driberg was right behind him, standing at the edge, scowling, attempting to pull at the boy's jacket. But his companion would not come down; instead, he snaked his arm around Colin's waist and they duetted at the microphone. When it was time for the final, stridently melodramatic line, Colin gamely attempted a full octave leap, maintained with an uncertain trill.

The song was over. The noise was deafening. Colin made an elaborate curtsey, incidentally disclosing that his frock had some sort of gossamer train, which fishtailed out to the side as he took hold of it with his right hand. If he was irritated at this incursion from the audience, Colin didn't show it. The boy attempted a bow of his own. Driberg angrily climbed up on the stage and grasped the boy's forearm. The boy wrenched it away and clung on to Colin's waist, as Colin continued to beam and bask in the applause. The boy kissed his cheek to cheers and, to more cheers, Colin kissed his new friend's forehead. They held hands, took a bow together and then, almost without looking at him, the boy planted a hand square in Driberg's chest – he had again clambered up – and shoved him back, so that he toppled over backwards into the arms of a now infuriated woman. The boy nuzzled Colin; they giggled together and then Driberg came back up to punch Colin, a blow which landed pointlessly on his shoulder. The piano accompaniment stopped as both men crashed off the stage to more roars from the onlookers.

Elizabeth saw Ginnie wading into the crowd, her tolerance clearly tested to its limits. With remarkable strength she wrenched Driberg and his assailant apart and made them shake hands. Then Elizabeth gave a start, as Mr Ware appeared from the back of the crowd, touched her arm and smiled ingratiatingly. He was now dressed entirely differently: in the uniform of an ARP officer. Many revellers noticed his clothing too, and gave cheers and toasts, saluting a civilian hero. These Mr Ware acknowledged with a gracious incline of the head. Tilting his helmet to a more rakish angle, he looked back at Elizabeth and grinned. Elizabeth looked away, and then at her watch. The woozy, unreal sensation from the smoke was now definitely receding, leaving behind it the first feelings of discontent with the present sensation and the first inklings of panic. The time had definitely come to go home. But how?

Colin was pushing his way through the throng, having stepped directly off the front of the stage, transparently keen to maximise the period in which he would be praised and congratulated by the crowd. Emerging after a discreet exit to his makeshift dressing room to get changed, might mean being ignored by an audience whose interest in him had long since evaporated. He was holding his wig in his hand, and that great bald head with its sweat, rouge, and bizarrely disproportionate hoop-earrings, was quite as offensive as anything Elizabeth had ever seen in her life. Nothing at the Windsor Castle Christmas pantomime had ever looked like this.

'I say, Lil, what did you think?' he said, as excited as a schoolboy.

'Oh, ah, awfully good,' said Elizabeth, looking at her watch again. 'Terribly good. Well done.'

'Thanks!' said Colin, satisfied with this. But his unselfconscious smile dimmed when Mr Ware now spoke to him.

'Yes. Terribly good, old cock. Are you going on again?'

'No, I don't think so. Why?'

'Well, I think you might as well. Because I think I don't need you on the venture I had in mind for this evening. And you were saying earlier you didn't feel like it.'

'What? Now, really —'

'Don't make a big song-and-a-dance about this, Colin. There might be something I can share with you later, but really this is a one-man job. Or rather, one-civilian job. The person I wish to accompany me will be a military type.' He directed his gaze archly to Elizabeth who, baffled, ignored him. Then he melted away back into the crowd. Where on earth was Mr Coward? Where was Katharine, come to think of it?

A young man came up to Colin, and whispered in his ear. Colin instantly grinned, perhaps expecting some congratulatory flirtation; his expression changed at once to disappointment, and then to alarm. Once the man had gone away, Colin looked feebly around and then turned to Elizabeth; apparently she was the only person to whom he could confide this new complication.

'I say, Lil,' he said, wheedlingly, 'I wonder if you could just pop into the Ladies'?'

'Why?' was all Elizabeth could manage to say.

'Because Katharine is in there. I'm sorry. She's had a spot of bother. Something of an upsetment. It's something that only a ... only a woman can really help with. Thanks!' he finished, brooking no demurral. He gestured fastidiously towards a door to the far side of the bar, well away from the stage, and melted away himself.

There was nothing else for it. Elizabeth pushed her way through the crowd, towards the ladies' lavatory. Perhaps Katharine was upset about something, perhaps she had

– Elizabeth cast about for an explanation – perhaps she had laddered a stocking. She would just give Katharine a bit of a pep talk and a cheer-up and then she would find Noël and get out of here.

She went through the door and, at the end of a passage, found two further doors. The only indication as to which was the ladies' was the fact that there was a large and intimidating man outside what was presumably the gentlemen's lavatory, preventing access, on the grounds that some sort of private altercation was in progress inside. Elizabeth could hear shoves and raised voices. Avoiding this man's eye, she pushed at the other entrance and went in.

Katharine was seated on a low wooden stool, by the handbasins. She was looking down, silent, with both hands up to her face.

'Katharine?' asked Elizabeth.

Her friend looked up, and Elizabeth saw that her left eye was red and swollen, a discolouration which extended up to her forehead, and that a tooth was missing.

'What happened? Who did that?' she asked at last.

Katharine did not answer at first. Then she said:

'He does it occasionally. I suppose I ask for it. I push him. I provoke him.'

'My *God*,' said Elizabeth, and then turned on a tap, intending to wash Katharine's bruised face. The first tap yielded nothing; a thin dribble was to be had from the next. There were no paper towels. Elizabeth cupped her hands and splashed water over Katharine's cheeks as best she could.

'I told him he should leave you alone,' said Katharine miserably. 'I said you should just be allowed to go home. It was my job to find a woman in uniform, you see?'

Elizabeth did not see. She wondered if she could just clean Katharine up, and then make an exit. Instantly, she reproved herself for such a uncharitable and un-Christian thought.

'So,' she hazarded, 'you met some man, some blackguard, and he's …' Her voice dropped in volume. '… knocked you about.'

The words felt bizarre on her lips. She had only the smallest notion of how such an event could take place. She understood that Katharine was married, and the censorious part of her guessed that this was the sort of thing that might well happen if you had casual meetings with someone who was not your husband. But then she had casually met people this evening, met them in a way she never would have dreamed of doing on any other night. Did that mean she herself was at risk of being 'knocked about'?

'Listen, Katharine,' Elizabeth said, and paused, wondering if she should give her a sisterly hug. She then did so, kneeling down, embracing her awkwardly as she sat. Katharine returned the embrace, sniffling quietly. She was silently ashamed to realise that she had no intention of calling the police, or allowing this situation to compromise her. Things had clearly got out of control, and Elizabeth now intended to make as clean a break as she could.

'Listen. Katharine,' she resumed, 'I want you to ... to buck up, and to come with me. I'm sure I can get a cab home and drop you off wherever you want to go. This evening has been jolly good fun, or at least it mostly has, and I'm sure we've all been doing things we wouldn't normally, but the time has come now to go home. You should just go home. You, oh.'

Elizabeth had to back away hurriedly as Katharine lurched to her feet, clamped a hand over her mouth, retched unproductively over a handbasin and then spat a mouthful of blood into it. Then she turned back.

'I know who you are,' she said.

'What?'

'I said, I know who you are.'

'Oh.'

'I always wondered what it would be like if I ever met you, like this, and it turns out to be like going out shopping with my mother, on a Saturday, and meeting one of my teachers in a shop.'

'When did you realise?'

'When you said all that about Margaret Lockwood.'

'Well, it's jolly nice of you not to – not to tell anyone. Are you sure you're all right?'

'I'm sure that I'm not all right. But I keep telling you, it's you I'm worried about.'

'Don't worry about me. You'll be perfectly all right, you know, once your husband comes home.'

'No, no. It was my husband that did this to me.'

Elizabeth now registered that Katharine's accent had descended the class scale.

'What? He's come *back*? Where is he?'

'He's here. You've spent the whole evening with him, you silly mare.' Katharine's swollen, leaden face turned on Elizabeth and accentuated the unthinkable insult with a sullen glare. 'It's William. *He's* my husband.'

Elizabeth's mouth opened, and at first couldn't reply. She swallowed and said, 'You mean – Ware? Mr Ware?'

'Yes.'

'And he's the one who has treated you like this?'

She did not hear the door open behind her.

'Yes.'

'So everything you've told me … isn't true?'

The door banged open and Elizabeth turned around. Katharine looked down.

'Sorry to come in here,' said Mr Ware easily. 'I couldn't get into the gents. A fellow seems to be standing guard out there; some sort of disagreement in progress therein.' He gave Katharine a soiled handkerchief, and she wordlessly pressed it against her cheek, which was now beginning to balloon in such a way as to make speech all but impossible. Widening his own mouth as if to yawn, he picked a fragment of cigarette paper from his lower lip and spoke again:

'In answer to your question, no, it's not true. We often work independently. Especially when it's up to my lady wife here to pick someone up, someone like you.'

'Pick someone *up*? But why?'

'Oh ...' slurred Katharine vaguely, quietly, almost to herself. 'jutht for, well, for fun, and thometimes William needth them for hith ARP work.'

'Your ARP work? Why on earth do you need to pick up a stranger for your ARP work?'

Mr Ware went into a lavatory stall and began to urinate. The noise was as loud as a chain being lowered onto a steel floor. 'You know, Lil ...' he said thoughtfully, speaking over his shoulder. 'You don't realise what goes on. We've all had it hard in London, during the Blitz. We haven't had enough food to eat. We've been asked to sacrifice. And you people, you high-ups, you haven't been asked to sacrifice a single bit.'

He came out, zipping himself up, not washing his hands, looking her in the eye. Elizabeth now considered that her best approach was to humour this man, to get herself out of this awful situation as quickly as possible. But her training, her idealism, her patriotism, all made it impossible to say anything other than the following:

'That's not true. Rationing has been for everyone.'

'That's a lie. A rotten lie.' Mr Ware now eyed her coldly, perceptibly ratcheting up his defiance and aggression. Elizabeth wondered if he, like Katharine, knew who she was.

'Yes, yes, you had rationing,' he continued. 'You've had the coupons. Oh dear, yes. But you've got cash, and rationing never mattered for you well-off types. You can go to restaurants any time you want. You can get all the food you want. You can stuff your faces, and you did. Can *I*? Can *she*?' His voice became shrill and he pointed to Katharine, who cringed into her clothes. 'So don't give me any of that old moody, Lil,' he said. 'Don't give me any of that old flannel. You folk have been protected in this war. Insulated. It's the East End that got the brunt of it.'

Elizabeth attempted to assert herself. 'That's all perfectly true, Mr Ware, and I entirely see your point, but now I have to—'

Mr Ware placed the palm of his hand square in Elizabeth's chest, and shoved hard enough for her to topple backwards onto Katharine.

'You just hold your horses, missy. You just settle down.'

Elizabeth slithered off Katharine, moving to the side, not certain that this manoeuvre would not provoke another assault. No one had treated her like this in her life. Her father had never struck her, and even Margaret would not presume to show such familiarity.

'Will you kindly allow me to pass?'

All Mr Ware did in response to this was light a cigarette and flick away the spent match so that it struck her on the cheek. She could feel the tiny, disagreeable sting of its heat, but proudly suppressed the impulse to bring her fingers up to her face.

She repeated:

'I now wish to leave. Will you kindly ...'

Katharine began, feebly, 'William, don't go to that houthe, pleathe no, 'thpecially not with her. Perhapth you'd better jutht ...'

'*You*,' he shrieked at her, a syllable that extended for two distinct, indignant notes, dipping down in tone. '*You* can belt up. *You* can keep your nose out. No one invited you. No one asked you. You can stay here. While Lil and I get this thing done.'

Mastering her fear and her rage, Elizabeth decided the time had come for the ultimate question.

'Do you know who I am?' she asked him, drawing herself up to her full height and squaring her shoulders. Katharine gave a tiny whimper.

Mr Ware looked disconcerted. He leant forward and looked into her face with a theatrically baffled frown, as if to ask, not who this young woman was, but what sort of young woman could dare to attempt intimidating him with such a ridiculous line. Then he looked closer, and then suddenly looked away, down to his left shoe, considering something, perhaps the identity of some entirely hypothetical person on whose behalf his wife might conceivably risk a battering from him. His head jerked back to look at Elizabeth and his eyes widened. Then he jumped back, gave a little, high laugh like a mouse-squeak, and brought his palms together as if in prayer, then up to his open mouth.

'William,' moaned Katharine, 'you'll thwing for this, you'll—'

The music had resumed outside, and the drumroll and cymbal clash coincided with the second, brutal slap Mr Ware gave Mrs Ware. Elizabeth jumped forwards, but Mr Ware had removed the Luger from his ARP bag and now it was in her face, the gun barrel almost touching her nose.

'Your Royal *Highness*?'

Twelve

Elizabeth left the lavatory with Mr Ware close behind her, the gun jammed into the small of her back. He had already told her: the slightest false move from her, the slightest attempt to warn anyone, to cry out, and she would 'get it'.

'Just stay calm,' he had told her, grimly. 'Don't act out of character and draw attention to yourself. Don't try and smile. You haven't been smiling the rest of the evening, Gawd only knows. Just looking as if you were at a fucking funeral.'

Was that true? Elizabeth thought she had been smiling benignly and attractively the entire time. Her mouth went into a thin, stretched, trembly line, the way it went when she was upset as a small child. Everything in her life was far away from her now: her parents, her sister, Philip. She saw it as if through the wrong end of a telescope.

They came out of the corridor, through the bar and back into the club. The point of the gun was sometimes pressed directly onto one of her vertebrae, and sometimes into the space in between. Literally everyone in the club was now attempting to dance, sloppy and careless.

Driberg came over. He had Colin with him and another boy, a different boy, slight, dark, with a sleepy-lidded look and a thin fuzz of a moustache.

'My dear!' Driberg called genially to her. 'Where have you been? Do you want to come with us? We're going to the Brown Bomber in Wardour Street. I am a member, you know. They serve a rather tasty bacon sandwich. Pickled onions. It's so much less formal than this.'

A man in his late sixties wearing a vivid yellow fright wig

lurched forwards between them and attempted to vomit on the floor.

'You see, *this* is what I am talking about,' said the dark, slight boy who had a slight Spanish accent. Colin nodded, but continued to look at Elizabeth.

The entire group moved a pace or two to the left to dissociate themselves from this man. Elizabeth felt the gun continue to jab into her spine. Driberg noticed how Mr Ware seemed to stay unnaturally close behind her back.

'Are you ... leaving us, Lil?' he presumed to ask.

'Yes, I think it's past my bedtime,' replied Elizabeth in a voice no one could hear. But they saw her smile and nod.

'And where are you off to, old boy?' Driberg said to Mr Ware, more sharply. 'And why on earth have you got that kit on?'

'I'm off myself,' he returned. 'Thought I might have a stroll up Hyde Park way. I was going to get Lil here a cab outside the Criterion.'

This seemed to satisfy the assembled company. Elizabeth felt Mr Ware remove the Luger from her back, and it had presumably gone back inside his waistband as he gestured broadly with his free hand around, but not touching, her shoulders, guiding her to the exit.

'Goodbye!' he said. 'See you in the morning, just when day is dawning!'

Elizabeth saw that now was her chance. He had had to put the gun away so that no one would see it. He had no power over her, but once they were out on the street, with no one else around, she would have no chance. He could do what he liked then. She would have to act now, right now. But do what? Scream? Cry out?

The drunk man with the yellow wig groaned, got to his feet, and began to stumble for the door by the bar, undoubtedly heading for the lavatory. Mr Ware's hand was gently on her shoulder again. Now. Do something now.

'There's Noël,' she said, suddenly. 'Noël!'

Coward had appeared out of the crowd, now really holding a

glass of champagne. Her high, yelping monosyllable should have been all but inaudible, but Coward's extra-sensory awareness of social importance made him stop and break off a conversation he was having with two other younger men. He approached and addressed her with rather more of the facetious gallantry than had seemed appropriate earlier in the evening.

'Ah, Lil,' he said, bowing, 'we were thinking of going to the Brown Bomber Club. One was hoping to discover how it got its name. One has the most appalling suspicions. Perhaps you would like to come along?'

'Oh,' said Elizabeth weakly, 'Yes, thank you, Noël, I—'

But from the other side of the room, and behind Coward, Elizabeth could now see Katharine, with her bruised and battered face. It looked like a boy's face, or a man's face, and Elizabeth could see where the tooth was missing: it was the swelling and distension of her cheek which revealed this gap.

Elizabeth remembered how shocked she had been when she saw this injury in the ladies' room, and how quickly and thoroughly she had suppressed the shock, but now remembered something else, another experience which she had suppressed, or which she had allowed events to suppress for her. She remembered kissing Katharine. She remembered how her tongue had found its way into that mouth; she had tasted gin and inhaled the intimate fume of cigarettes which she associated with her father. Elizabeth had probed Katharine's teeth with her tongue. She had not especially meant to, but there seemed no other osculatory way to behave while their mouths were locked together. It was like making conversation. The top row of Katharine's teeth really were very close to her top lip. Philip's teeth were not, in fact, like that. She did not remember feeling them with her tongue or lips when they kissed, although there was actually the same tobacco smell. Was that what she was remembering? If she kissed Katharine now, Elizabeth thought, her tongue would feel that broken stump of a tooth, feel it as a flinty point or as something hollow, like a straw.

Elizabeth felt woozy. Her field of vision seemed to have a

metallic shimmer or glitter that she could taste. She wondered if she should faint – pretend to faint, or really faint, and that would get her out of a jam. And yet the realisation that this might indeed be a good idea, seemed to cure her passing infirmity. She no longer felt in the slightest like fainting. An ingrained refusal to give in, a determination to buck up, stopped it happening. As for pretending to pass out, it was somehow utterly beyond her as well.

Noël gently repeated his offer about the Brown Bomber club, and Elizabeth numbly realised that a loud and sweeping acceptance, a ringing and comically imperious 'Oh yes! Take me away from here!' – the sort of line Margaret could probably deliver – would solve all her problems at once. But she just couldn't do it. As if in a dream, she couldn't speak. Having first assented, the momentum of what was happening seemed unstoppable. She smiled and shook her head at Coward, who graciously inclined his own in return, taking it on the chin.

After all, this man had a gun, didn't he? Everyone knew, from films and suchlike, that when someone produced a gun you had to do what they said. Elizabeth, muddled, had quite forgotten about her conviction that he would be afraid to use the gun now.

There was something else, too. Elizabeth turned Noël Coward down because she was accustomed to declining, to refusing, gracefully shying away when members of the public asked her questions, or made approaches of any sort, and this instinct made her smile, and shake her head and look down. In any case, to reveal to these people, people with whom she had crassly attempted to mix socially, that she had put herself in this position – it was unthinkable. No, once they were out on the street, she would hail a cab. No, she would hail a policeman. She would hail a cab *and* a policeman. She would run away. Elizabeth could see Katharine talking to Ginnie, and Ginnie looking over to them, and then reaching for the telephone on one of the glass shelves behind the bar. She could feel a weakness and a sagging at the knees, and Mr Ware's grip across her shoulders grew suddenly tighter.

'Come on, now.'

They left the Club, out through the throng. Up the steps, through the trapdoor device and back up onto the streets of Soho. The cold air and the noise, the different sort of noise, made Elizabeth feel nauseous and faint. Now his grip on her elbow was powerfully strong. There were no cabs anywhere.

'Let's walk,' said Mr Ware. He had lit another cigarette; this was clamped in the corner of his mouth, and he had adopted a ventriloquist's way of talking, looking straight ahead, hardly moving his lips. What was the point? Nobody was looking at them. Elizabeth's heart leapt as she saw a policeman approach: a big, cheerful, ruddy face under his helmet.

'Evening to you both,' he said pleasantly, with a slight West Country accent. 'What are you in your kit for? Don't you know there's *not* a war on?'

All three laughed at his playful sally.

'Oh, I've got some properties to inspect, chief. My work is never done.'

'You're a glutton for it!'

'Certainly!'

'And what about you, miss?' he asked, easily. 'Have you got to help?'

'Oh yes,' she smiled. Here was a policeman. Exactly what she wanted, and yet when she opened her mouth to speak, the words would not come.

'Well, keep out of trouble. Good night all.'

He stalked off up northward, in the direction of Oxford Street. They walked on down Shaftesbury Avenue and into Piccadilly Circus: a young woman in uniform, still neatly turned out, and someone from the ARP, in his vivid white helmet and kitbag. They attracted attention here and there. People called out to them, but Mr Ware maintained his grip and Elizabeth could still feel the butt of his gun in her back. Two women walked past, gobbling fish and chips from a newspaper.

'I'm hungry,' said Elizabeth.

'Come on. Just keep moving.'

'I'm hungry. I've got to have some food, or I think I'm going to faint.'

'Didn't you have anything at the club?'

Passers-by probably thought they were sweethearts, or a married couple.

'There wasn't anything.'

Mr Ware and Elizabeth were now actually standing outside an Italian café.

'I am going to faint. I haven't eaten anything for hours. Not since lunch.'

Mr Ware looked at his watch, and then frowningly at Elizabeth.

'All right. We'll stop in here. You can have a sandwich and a cup of tea. Something like that. Ten minutes, maximum.'

A listless older woman and a young girl, so similar she had to be a granddaughter, stood behind the counter. Elizabeth sat at one of the tables, and looked around at the other customers. A young man, unshaven, dirty, hunched over a single cup of coffee. He did not look up. Another group of young men, with what appeared to be the remnants of facepaint and eye makeup gathered, giggling among themselves, at a further table.

What on earth was she going to do? Should she call the police? Yes, surely, that was what she must do. He wouldn't dare use his gun now, in broad view of everyone. She should call the police, right now. Elizabeth imagined her thin, scared, cracked voice suddenly breaking the low, grumbling quiet. She imagined her desperate scream for help. Would these people help her? Would they recognise her? If they did, might it not actually lessen her chances of being helped? People would be astonished, unbelieving. They would not credit that it was up to them to protect their future Queen. They would not believe that someone of her class could possibly get herself into this situation. They might think it was some sort of stunt or hoax. Each of them, individually, would think that it was someone else's responsibility to do something about it. Miserably, frantically, her thoughts running like a hamster on a wheel, Elizabeth realised how paralysed she felt.

Mr Ware was selecting sandwiches and a bun. The woman behind the counter was preparing a pot of tea for two.

What did he want her for? Elizabeth thought about this question for the first time, realised that she did not know and how scared this thought made her.

Mr Ware was putting the sandwiches, the bun and the tea onto a tray, and preparing to carry them over himself, apparently forestalling the woman's suggestion that the young girl should do it.

Something about this whole situation was familiar to her. Quite aside from the danger and the squalor of the situation into which she had got herself so badly messed up, a long buried memory was beginning to stir. Could it be that she visited this café long ago, as a child? Or a café like this?

Mr Ware arrived at their table, his tray trembling and rattling with the weight. With a *chink*, he placed it heavily down.

'Right. There you are.'

He sat down opposite her, sweating. His ARP helmet was now tipped back on his head, in a parody of rakishness.

'I'll be mother, shall I?'

He poured the tea, and shoved her sandwiches towards her.

'There you are. Chicken. Very nice. Actually cost me more than I thought. But never mind. I'm going to be quids in, after tonight. You're going to help.'

'What are you going to do?' Elizabeth finally got the question out, after much effort.

'What are *we* going to do, you mean!' he said smugly. 'You and I are going to do some war work, my dear. The last bit of war work of the war. What do you think *this* is about?' He tapped the helmet with a forefinger, and then lit another of his odd-shaped cigarettes.

'What sort of war work?' Elizabeth asked, now hoping to humour him.

'Important war work. Vital war work. Home front work. Very important to the maintenance of civilian morale.'

'Civilian morale?'

'My morale, darling, my morale, and I'm a civilian. This work for the ARP has got me into some pretty dangerous situations, you know. Well, I don't suppose you do know. Your sort just swan about, in no danger at all.'

'That's not true.'

Mr Ware's manner reverted to his previous cold scorn.

'Listen to me, Lil,' he said. 'People have died in this war. People got killed from Jerry's bombs here: every night. It's been bloody chaos. Bloody anarchy. Nightfall to sunup. Do you think we've all been fucking cheery Cockneys getting on with it and whistling while we work and keeping our peckers up? Well, we haven't. The things I've seen while I've been seeing to bombed out houses. While I've been pulling dead bodies out of the dust. Women. Children. In that sort of situation, people don't care. There's no law and order.'

Now he took out the Luger and slammed it down on the table, while keeping the flat of his hand on the weapon, partially concealing it. No one else in the café looked up or showed the slightest interest. Furious rows between men and women were entirely commonplace here.

'I've had to use this a couple of times, and not on Fritz. Had to. Do you think the police were going to help us, in London during the Blitz? We just had to police ourselves.'

'What do you mean, use it?'

'Are you getting cheeky?'

Mr Ware paused, removed his gun from the table, sipped his tea and nibbled the bun, keeping his bloodshot eyes warily and resentfully on Elizabeth.

'People here have just had to help themselves as best they could. God helps those who help themselves, doesn't he? And I've been helping myself. We all have. Those as could. Round here, some places got on the end of V-2s. Last one landed only recently. People are still clearing up the mess; the likes of me are clearing it up. D'you know what V-2s are?'

Elizabeth did, but didn't speak.

'It's a type of Jerry rocket-bomb. I'm not surprised you don't know anything about them. Do you know what the V stands for?'

Again, Elizabeth said nothing.

'Well, let me tell you. Let me put you in the picture. The V stands for Vergeltungswaffe. I read that in the paper. Ver-gelt-ungs-waffe. It means revenge weapon. I can understand that. Revenge weapon. I've got one myself.' He patted the Luger.

Suddenly Mr Ware's thoughtful indignation gave way to the cunning grin that had been his default position all evening. He sat back, smirking at her, smoking the cigarette that made his pupils dilate and turned his eyes into two faintly irregular discs, like dirty threepenny bits.

Elizabeth rallied.

'What on earth do you think is going to happen to you after this? Do you know who I am?' she repeated.

He smiled, as if she was joking, or as if she was using her resemblance to a celebrated person, combined with her class superiority, in order to cow him. Did he realise who she was, or not?

'Werll ...' said Mr Ware expansively. 'Your Royal Highness. You've gone slumming it in London's streets. That club had some pretty nasty pieces of work in it. You saw some of your chums, I noticed. You ask them the things that go on. Make your hair curl. But you know it's all basically just fun. Bit of horseplay. Nothing really bad happened, did it?'

Elizabeth thought about Katharine's face: her broken tooth, and what it was like kissing her, before it was broken. The memory flashed in and out of her mind, like a glimpsed photograph in the turning pages of someone else's magazine.

'And William Ware, ARP officer, accompanied you to safety,' he continued. 'On your way home, you were able to help me with my war work. After this night's over, you can just forget about it all. I thought you were supposed to be hungry, by the way.'

He smoked his cigarette again, and his pupils appeared to get darker and deeper. Elizabeth obediently tried to eat her chicken sandwich. She chewed the pieces of food, found there was no way of swallowing them, expelled them back into her paper napkin as discreetly as she could and took another sip of her tea.

'I think I wish to be excused,' she said at last.

Mr Ware simply frowned.

'I wish to go to the lavatory.'

He grunted. 'All right, then. There it is. Mind you're not long.'

Elizabeth went round, past the café counter, and tried to catch the eye of the woman serving and the younger girl. Both resolutely looked away. They were closing up soon.

In the tiny lavatory, Elizabeth saw what she had been both hoping and dreading to find: a small open window. By hitching up her skirt and standing on one of the handbasins, she was able to look out. The window faced onto a tiny yard, with three big dustbins with lids just below. There appeared to be a passage leading away from the yard and round a corner. Where that led, she had no idea. Perhaps to freedom, perhaps to a brick wall.

She heard the bark of a dog, reasonably near.

Elizabeth pressed her hand to her forehead, as if taking her own temperature. She tensed her haunches, about to climb down, then changed her mind and stayed where she was. The dog had stopped barking. She could hear the hiss from the café's tea urn. It was now or never.

She squeezed herself through the window, and found herself almost, but not quite, trapped around the waist. There was no way to straighten up and kneel or crouch on the sill: the window was hardly larger than a ship's porthole. The more she got herself through, the more emphatically she jack-knifed in the middle, with the crown of her head pointing almost directly down at the ground. After squirming and wriggling back, and finally retreating from the window-frame, she made another attempt, this time pushing her head and both hands through the enclosed space at once; she was now able to get palms, forearms and elbows out through the window-frame, her shoulders jammed against her ears. Again, she tilted downwards, her tummy flat on the sill underneath. With both hands, Elizabeth pressed on the brickwork beneath her; it was the only way to advance. There was no way to control her eventual landing. She would just have to push and push herself out, and when she began to topple, and gravity took over, the only thing to do was to stretch out her fingertips, and hope that her descent onto the dustbins would not be too loud or too painful. Would she break her arms? Would she break her neck? The hiss from the café now gave way to shouts in the kitchen. She had to get on with it.

Elizabeth pushed forwards, and dropped. Falling through the air seemed to take a microsecond longer than she thought, enough to register her skirts ballooning around her waist. And then, crash! Her palms entirely failed to lessen the blow of her forearms and skull against the metal discs and Elizabeth did an agonising and – she could still sense it – horrendously undignified forward roll, and landed on her back, into which the bin's raised edge now dug excruciatingly.

She had never wanted anything in her life more than she wanted to cry – both to cry out, and to cry, to weep with pure pain and fear. Her head, back, arms and pelvis were in serious pain. Had she broken anything? No. She could move. She was all right. She relaxed. She almost luxuriated, absurdly, in this position, like a tailor's dummy dropped from an aeroplane onto a semi-upturned dustbin. The dog had started barking again and she could hear raised voices from inside the café. There was no choice but to keep moving. Elizabeth got up and started to run to where she could see the passageway turning, then buckled slightly and almost fell with the renewed pain, and then rallied and kept moving, a continuous movement in which she appeared to crouch down and straighten in mid-gallop.

Around the corner was a high, locked gate, with six vertical metal posts, bisected by two diagonals, angled from the top left to bottom right: the higher was at the level of her face, the lower at the level of her knees. The dog was chained up in a neighbouring yard. Elizabeth realised that its breathing was as laboured as hers.

She began to climb the gate. Her left foot went in, higher than her right, on the sloping lower bar. Agonisingly, each instep was crushed into the metal by the angle. Pushing off from the left, she tried to hoist her right foot up onto the upper bar and with her right hand grabbed one of the row of topmost rails, exposed like spikes. Elizabeth sagged at this stage, and hoisted up her skirts around her waist, to give herself more room to move. With a superhuman heave, she managed to get herself up on the top of the gate, and found that the spikes were spaced just widely enough to allow Elizabeth to squeeze her bottom down between them and sit astride it.

The dog looked up and began to bark again.

Now Elizabeth swung her other leg over and found that she had, from this vantage point, no easy way of judging where the footholds and handholds were going to be on the way down. And it really did look like a long drop. Her body continued to tremble and shudder in a way that made the whole gate rattle. Elizabeth could now hear the back door into the yard open and someone begin to turn the bins the right side up. They would know she had made her escape through the window. They would come round looking for her. She would have to jump, would have to do it now. At least it wasn't a case of landing headfirst.

Elizabeth swung back and forth, and then leapt off. Her impact on the pavement was obscured by another deafening bark from the dog. She bent at the knees in an attempt to lessen the impact, but an excruciating pain seared both ankles.

Elizabeth could hear footsteps.

She got up and attempted to run. Her whole upper body was shaking; her lungs were burning, and the pain in her ankles meant she ran with a crazy, wobbling, splayed gait. Rounding the corner, wheezing but still not crying with distress, she found her way into another small yard, which led back round into Piccadilly. She was free – wasn't she?

Staggering, Elizabeth found herself back on the main street. She was opposite the Royal Academy: actually, some way west of it. She reeled, and fought a desire a vomit. Every bodily movement exacerbated the pain she felt everywhere. Frantically, Elizabeth looked up and down the pavement – all she could see were stragglers and drunk people. She could not see Mr Ware. Was there a taxi? No. Eerily, there were no vehicles, no private cars, just people stumbling and drifting over the wide avenue.

Suddenly, Elizabeth saw a policeman, a man with precisely that genial, tolerant and yet watchful look that she saw in the officer who had accosted them both when she left the club. Seeing her, the man appeared instantly to break into a broad, welcoming smile. It was a good omen. She attempted a bleary smile of her own and stumbled over towards him, asking for his help, as loudly as she could, over and over, well before he had any chance of hearing what on earth she was actually saying.

'Now, now, then,' said the constable tolerantly, 'what's all this? One too many, is it? All over the place, you are.'

Elizabeth almost collapsed into his arms, gasped for breath, attempted to say the word 'help' but only retched into her palms.

'Oh dear, oh dear,' he smiled, with more severity now. 'This is no behaviour for someone in uniform, VE Night or no VE Night. I suggest you get yourself on home.'

Elizabeth's face became a grimacing mask, still she could not catch her breath. 'It … it …'

'Is this young lady with you, sir?' asked the policeman, looking at someone just behind Elizabeth's right shoulder, and she could now feel the Luger jammed once again into the small of her back.

'Yes, sir, I'm sorry about this. We've all been making rather merry.'

The sycophancy of Mr Ware's way of speaking, coupled with that quaint Dickensian phrase, made Elizabeth almost sag at the knees with horror and disgust. She did in fact collapse slightly, and Mr Ware grabbed her under the left armpit while keeping the gun barrel firmly jammed in position.

'Will you be all right?' asked the policeman.

'Oh yes, oh yes, please don't worry about us. I've got her now. It's time to call it a night. It's been quite a night, hasn't it?'

At this moment, a taxi came past with its light on. Mr Ware smartly placed his thumb and forefinger in his pursed mouth and gave a piercing whistle.

'We'll be off now.'

They were bundling into the back of the cab when the constable said quietly, and ineffectually, 'Wait a bit, aren't you ...?'

From inside the cab, Elizabeth looked back at the shrinking image of the officer with his puzzled, suspicious face.

Thirteen

'Not long, now, Lil,' said Mr Ware. 'Not long. I just need you along with me for this job, and then, when the sun comes up, you can go back to your life and I can go back to mine.'

They had got out of the taxi at the Western end of Green Street in Mayfair, opposite Speaker's Corner. A row of houses were badly bomb-damaged, and boarded up. A single policeman stood outside to guard against looters, looking sleepy and resentful, holding a cigarette with the lighted tip inward into his palm.

'Evening, or should I say, morning!' said Mr Ware, stepping up to him briskly with a broad smile.

'Yes? What can I do for you?'

'We just have to retrieve some equipment I've left behind.'

'What sort of equipment?'

'Two gas masks, a fire axe and my colleague's whistle,' continued Mr Ware brightly. 'Left in there when we inspected this property last Monday. Got to account for all the equipment, you know. Very important we get it all back. It's a military matter,' he added knowingly, pointing at Elizabeth. 'My colleague is coming with me to establish that it's all present and correct.

'Where's this kit of yours stowed?' asked the officer, quite baffled, but too weary to argue.

'Ground floor.'

'Well, for Gawd's sake mind you don't try going upstairs. The bomb damaged the stairwell; the thing's unstable and the whole kaboodle could come down if you're not very careful.'

'Right you are, chief.'

'Don't be in there long.'

'Wouldn't dream of it.'

There was another moment of hesitation and then the policeman exhaled heavily, puffing out his cheeks, let them through the door-sized hole sawn into the boarding, drawing aside a sheet of tarpaulin like a curtain. The second level of admission to the house was the battered and unsecured front door, which opened when Mr Ware shoved against it. It ground against the rubble and rubbish strewn about the floor, but swung back eventually. Mr Ware pushed Elizabeth inside and produced a torch from his bag; he removed his gun as well and held it in his other hand, pointing it at Elizabeth.

'Don't you cry out, my girl,' he told her. 'Don't you fucking make a peep. This is it. We're here now. We're in! Isn't this a thrill?'

He laid the Luger down on a surface, apparently a sideboard, and swung the torch beam around. Then he moved forward, as stealthily as a cat.

'Yes,' he breathed, 'there we are. There's the kitchen. You can see the sink. There's the kettle. Most of the wall's gone, you see.'

Elizabeth could see the rough lumber of the wooden boarding behind the jagged expanse of missing wall. Most of the kitchen floor, she could see, was covered in a mound of rubble that could have been about knee-height if you tried to stand in it. She could see what looked like a smashed rocking chair on one side, whose wooden back-struts had come away, and a ruined couch at the other end, with some cushions lying about. Elizabeth was also aware of a strange, sweetish smell.

'V2 hit this place. One and only V2 to make the West End! I happened to be on the scene. They cleared us all out sharpish, and I happen to know they didn't look for survivors. And why? Because, for why, they'd been informed there were *no* survivors. By yours truly. Tonight's the first chance I've had to get back in here, and to be quite honest, I didn't know if they were going to let me back in at all. Bringing along someone in uniform was my insurance policy.' In the darkness, Elizabeth could just see Mr Ware wink. 'All right.

Come on then,' he said, pointing his torch up into the corner, where the stairs were. 'Up we go. This is where we strike a rich seam, my girl! Get along with you,' he picked up the Luger and shoved it into Elizabeth's back. From somewhere, she found the courage to speak.

'But, didn't he say we weren't to go up there? That the whole building might come down?'

'Oh, for Christ's sake. Just fucking get on with it. Would I do this if it wasn't safe? Would I? Of course not! Come on.'

Gingerly, Elizabeth placed a foot upon the first stair, and then the next upon the second. Minutely, but distinctly, the whole staircase began to creak, and seemed to list about a sixteenth of an inch to the left. A fine spray of dust, as if from a bottle of sal volatile, floated down from somewhere up above and settled on her hair and forehead.

'Oh my God,' gasped Elizabeth, starting to feel faint, 'we can't do this. Please. We mustn't do this. It's all going to collapse.'

'Come on. Get on with it.'

Very slowly, and as if traversing a narrow, swaying rope bridge, Elizabeth and Mr Ware climbed the stairs, which stayed steady. A fine, powdery dust continued to fall. At the top, they found themselves on a narrow landing, which was dimly illuminated by the dawn light through the window. The beam of Mr Ware's torch swung round and picked out the handle of the door on their left. He twisted it; the door opened easily and they were in.

The window had been blown out and there was broken glass and rubbish in a mound over a double bed. Mr Ware gave Elizabeth the torch.

'Hold this. Point it at the bed.'

Greedily, hastily, and apparently all but forgetting that Elizabeth was there, Mr Ware scrabbled away at what covered the bed. Within a minute, he had disclosed an eiderdown, under which were two dead bodies: that of a man and a woman. The man was in pyjamas, the woman in a nightgown. Their heads, and the pillows on which they rested, had turned black. The

sweetish smell that Elizabeth could sense on the lower floor of
the house intensified almost unbearably.

Mr Ware scrambled round to the woman's side of the bed,
gesturing brusquely to Elizabeth to keep the torch trained on
him; numbly, she complied. He wrenched back the eiderdown
and the sheet and tried to pull out the woman's hand. This was
not easy. Rigor mortis had set in: it was like pulling at the arm
of a statue. But he was able to get a grip on it, and Elizabeth
could see that there were rings on almost every finger except the
thumb. One had what looked like a diamond. Mr Ware
scrabbled in his bag and produced a pot of Vaseline. Frantically,
he rubbed at the dead, stiff fingers and, with practised skill,
removed every ring and carefully stowed them in the pouch of
a wallet which he took from his pocket.

'Beautiful,' he whispered. 'I knew it. Beautiful. Now, then.
Let's have a look at the other hand.'

But there were no rings on that one. Mr Ware shrugged, and
went round to the other side of the bed, and quickly took
possession of the dead man's gold signet ring, using the Vaseline
pot, as before.

'Right,' he said simply, and then began systematically to open
the drawers of a bedside cabinet, starting with the one at the
bottom, so he wouldn't have to waste time closing each one.
When it came to the top-most drawer, he gasped, while
removing a small case from what looked like a sweater.

'Oh Jesus, Lil. Oh Jesus.'

He opened up the case and took out what appeared in the
blackness to be a cord.

'Keep that bloody light steady on me, girl!'

She did so, and the beam picked out a gorgeous dazzle. Mr
Ware bunched the necklace in his fist and stuffed it back inside
the case, so roughly that, at first, the lid would not shut properly.
Elizabeth then saw him grow strangely still. He appeared to be
thinking about something.

'Put the torch beam on my mouth,' he said quietly.

'What?'

'Just do it.'

Elizabeth shone the torch onto his mouth, and Mr Ware grinned, pulling his lips back, like a skull.

'Look!' he said brightly. 'All my baby teeth. All of them. Never dropped out when I was a kid. All of them. All my baby teeth.'

For a few seconds, Mr Ware did his death's-head grin in the darkness. Then he snapped out of it. 'All right, let's go,' he said curtly. 'We've got to go. We've got to quit while we're ahead. Can't risk staying here any longer. Let's go. Down the stairs, and out. Come on.'

He pushed Elizabeth ahead of him. She stepped forward, around the bed, and back out of the door, with her captor following. They stepped down the swaying stairs, and again a fine cloud of dust sprayed down on them in the darkness, dislodged by their disturbance to the house's damaged spinal column. Now there was an ominous groaning and creaking to the staircase as it tilted. Elizabeth was light-headed and dizzy as they reached the ground. They had to get out of there. But Mr Ware was reluctant to leave, perhaps suspecting there might be more treasure to be had, or else simply savouring the scene of his great triumph.

'You know, it's funny,' he mused. 'It's funny what Katharine was saying about you looking like – well, you know. What a joke. I almost believed it myself at first!'

Elizabeth said nothing. She just edged towards the door.

'How funny. How funny.' The thin shaft of daylight showed Mr Ware to be smiling delightedly, lost in thought.

'Shouldn't we go now?' Elizabeth asked.

'What? Oh. Oh, yes.'

They were about to make a move towards the door, when Elizabeth stopped. She could hear a faint whining sound, like a small animal in distress.

'Stop,' she said. 'Can you hear that?'

Mr Ware frowned at her, suspecting a trick. But then he heard it too. A tiny, all but inaudible moan. It seemed to be coming from the kitchen area behind them, the area buried in detritus. Mr Ware turned to look in the direction of the noise, then back to Elizabeth. He took out his gun again, and pointed it at her.

'Don't you try anything,' he snapped, and went around the detritus mound from where the noise appeared to be coming, squatted down on his haunches, removed his bag, placed it on the ground, and then placed his gun on top of that. He looked sharply up at Elizabeth, picked up the gun, made an ostentatious click on its safety catch and placed it down again, close by. Then he began to scoop the debris away with both hands, scoop, scoop, scoop. The noise got louder, and still louder. Scoop, scoop.

And then they saw it: what looked like a boy of eighteen or perhaps nineteen, half-buried in the dust, his face caked in white, the blackened rills of blood running along the side of his head, a fragment of what looked like toast pressed on his cheek, and placed in his slack lips, the spout of a big, unbroken teapot. Did the impact interrupt him as he carried tea and toast? Somehow, Mr Ware had overlooked this other occupant of the house, presumably the son of the couple upstairs. He was still alive. Again, the tiny, thin moan.

'Fetch me one of those cushions,' snapped Mr Ware. 'Fetch the bloody thing!' he repeated, as Elizabeth stood there dumbly. Pulling herself together, she stumbled over to where cushions were scattered on the floor, took one, brought it back and tremblingly gave it to him.

'Yes,' she said, 'perhaps if you put it under his head.'

Mr Ware knelt down beside the boy with the cushion in his hand, looking almost tender.

'You can make him comfortable, yes, but it would be far better to get him out of the rubble, before you get the cushion under his—'

Mr Ware gripped the cushion in both hands and pushed it down hard onto the boy's face. The soft low whining noise was replaced by an infinitesimally increased note of pain.

'No! You can't! You mustn't!'

Very quickly, there was silence. Mr Ware said, 'There.'

Elizabeth had now ceased to tremble. She turned white with rage. The whole night's disgust boiled up inside her, and exploded.

'You beast,' she said to him. 'You beast. You shameful, disgusting, unutterable beast.'

Mr Ware sneered and shrugged.

'Come on,' he said, and made to grab her. But Elizabeth ducked out of his grip, stumbled back to where the broken rocking chair was to be found, and picked up one of the wooden strut-poles, brandishing it at him.

'Put that down, Lil. Come on.'

'You beast. You horrible beast.'

'Put it down.'

The pole was heavier than she thought, more like a beam. The two of them squared warily up to each other. Elizabeth glanced at where he had left the gun on top of his kitbag.

'Get away from me.'

'Come on. Don't be a stupid girl. Come on.'

Suddenly, Elizabeth changed her grip on the beam, holding it at its end, as if she were tossing a caber, and shoved so that it shot outwards, as straight as a torpedo, straight into Mr Ware's face.

There was a crack, and a yelp of pain. Elizabeth dropped the pole. Mr Ware held both hands up to his mouth, from which blood was pouring. He put his hands down, and she could see that four of his teeth, two from the top and two from the bottom, had gone.

'Bissh,' he slobbered. 'Fughg bissh.'

Lunging forward, he made a move to grab her, but was too dazed to do this with any firmness or accuracy. It was a brief grapple as Elizabeth slithered past him, and desperately grabbed for the gun.

'Bisssh. Nogh.'

'Stay back. Stay back. I'm warning you.'

Elizabeth had picked up the Luger, and now, pale and

defiant, was holding it with both hands, arms outstretched, pointing the gun straight at him.

'Stay back or I shall have to shoot you,' she said. 'I mean it. Stay back.'

Mr Ware stayed where he was, swaying. His mouth was drawn back in a bloody, broken grimace and it was difficult to tell if he was sneering at her or not.

'Bissh. You.'

His mouth was now a broad, smudged oblong of blood.

Then, having apparently decided on something, he turned round and looked for something on the ground. He picked it up: the wooden pole that Elizabeth had just hit him with. Mr Ware held the end with two fists, one on top of each other, with the pole angled up high behind his head, like a baseball player.

'Stop. Get back. Stop,' said Elizabeth. The gun was now beginning to tremble.

'You. You. You.'

Mr Ware brought his bunched fists up over the crown of his head, and his weapon disappeared briefly behind his back; he was clearly preparing to smash it down onto Elizabeth's skull with all his might. He stepped forward, and Elizabeth took one pace back.

His face was now a mask of blood.

With a groan, he made to bring his club down on Elizabeth. She flinched, shut her eyes and fired three times.

Krak. Krak. Krak.

Elizabeth dropped the gun clatteringly onto the floor, her wrists in agony from the recoil.

Mr Ware continued to advance on her, swaying, but now sneering and gurgling and gloating in triumph, still with the club raised. He appeared to be shifting its position in his hands, waggling it, to get a better aim at his defenceless victim. He kept shuffling forward, and Elizabeth retreated, now utterly without hope. She sank down on her knees, her palms pressed on top of her head.

'You. You.'

But there was something odd about the way Mr Ware's body now twisted and jerked to the side, and the movement of his legs had a shuffling, uncoordinated manner, as if his pelvis were locked. This was because, though the first of Elizabeth's bullets had hit the wall behind him, the second had pierced his right forearm just above the elbow, and the third had entered his head three inches above his left eyebrow.

Mr Ware was quite still, but then lurched away, flailing blindly with outstretched, stiffened arms, like a swimmer, and crashed into the bottom of the staircase, tried vainly to heave himself up, and crashed down again. Instantly, there was a groaning and cracking from somewhere up above. The spray of dust from the upper storey had become a downpour. The ceiling bowed terrifyingly and a crack travelled down the wall.

Elizabeth stood up. Her knee-joints felt as though they were made of honey. She scrabbled out of the front door, past the tarpaulin, through the wooden door-hole. She got out into the street and scrambled and staggered away.

Behind her, she could hear the deafening, rending crash of the house collapsing in a shower of dirt and dust, motes of which were now beginning to circle round in front of her.

Elizabeth opened her mouth to scream but no sound came out.

Fourteen

The sound took quite a while to die away.

Elizabeth did not look round. She blinked, found her eyelashes had gummed together and prised them back open with her fingertips. Then she pushed her hair back from her forehead and smoothed down her skirts which had changed to the colour of dust.

She looked at her shoes: these too were very dirty.

Elizabeth realised that this was the first time she had ever stayed up all night.

She began to walk, listening to the birdsong. Should she take a cab? Should she take a bus? She heard traffic. There must be cabs.

Elizabeth would have liked somewhere to sit down, but there was no bench, or low wall. She pushed out her left hand and bent her elbow round, meaning to check the time. The watch-dial loomed blankly.

Her wrists both hurt a great deal and she realised that her ears were ringing. A brief, trembly movement with her right hand confirmed that she still had her purse.

She turned a corner, then hesitated, and looked back round to where she had come from.

She peered to the end of the street, which was still hazy with unsettled dust, like smoke from a bonfire. That policeman seemed to have vanished. No. There he was. Talking to a group of people in uniform, and pointing to her. Now they were walking quickly in her direction – running, actually.

She could see London's streets: houses, curtained windows. She could still hear distant merrymakers, who were still out in these streets. All those people, people drinking, people laughing, people fighting, people talking, all those people she had seen from the Palace balcony last night: all the same people. People everywhere.

Elizabeth coughed; her side hurt, she put her hand to the pain, bent over a little, and again found herself unable to check the movement. She was sinking back down to her knees, but found the strength to straighten when the men got close to her.

It was then that Elizabeth recognised Hugh, her VE Night gallant, in his uniform of the Scots Guards. But something queer had happened.

His blond hair had turned completely grey.

'Oh, Your Highness,' he gasped, presuming to take her hand. 'Your Royal Highness. Oh, thank God. Are you all right, Your Royal Highness?'

'Perfectly, thank you.'

'Oh, great merciful God and all the English saints and martyrs.'

Someone was now placing a blanket around her shoulders, and offering a sip of brandy in a metal cup from a hip flask. She waved it away. Hugh had some. All around her, Elizabeth could hear singing and screeching and shouting. She could hear the backfiring of cars, and even the tinkling of glass. And above it all, one distant voice:

'Victory in Japan! Victory in *Japan*! *Victory in Japan!*'

Acknowledgements

I offer fervent thanks to David Miller, Alex Goodwin, Jon Jackson, Peter Mayer, Robert Lacey, Jamie-Lee Nardone, Matt Nieman Sims, Linda Grant, Prof. Margot Gosney, Hugh Bonneville, Ben Liston and David Baddiel. As ever, extra special thanks are due to Caroline Hill.